"I Could Get Used To You, Chas,"

Amy said.

"Would that be so bad?"

"I'm not ready."

"I think we should explore this magic between us. It's like nothing I've ever experienced. Is it us? The weather? A spell? Would it last? We hardly know each other's names, and look at this miracle."

"It's only an interlude," she warned him. "Push, and we'll have to split now."

"You're a hard-nosed woman."

"See?" She smiled gently. "I'm not perfect."

"Close enough." He grinned at her.

Dear Reader,

As always, I am proud to be bringing you the very best that romance has to offer—starting with an absolutely wonderful *Man of the Month* from Annette Broadrick called *Mysterious Mountain Man*. A book from Annette is always a real treat, and I know this story—her fortieth for Silhouette—will satisfy her fans and gain her new ones!

As readers, you've told me that you *love* miniseries, and you'll find some of the best series right here at Silhouette Desire. This month we have *The Cop and the Chorus Girl*, the second book in Nancy Martin's delightful *Opposites Attract* series, and *Dream Wedding*, the next book in Pamela Macaluso's *Just Married* series.

For those who like a touch of the supernatural, look for Linda Turner's *Heaven Can't Wait*. Lass Small's many fans will be excited about her latest, *Impulse*. And Kelly Jamison brings us a tender tale about a woman who returns to her hometown to confront her child's father in *Forsaken Father*.

Don't miss any of these great love stories!

Lucia Macro,
Senior Editor

Please address questions and book requests to:
Silhouette Reader Service
U.S.: 3010 Walden Ave., P.O. Box 1325, Buffalo, NY 14269
Canadian: P.O. Box 609, Fort Erie, Ont. L2A 5X3

Lass Small
IMPULSE

SILHOUETTE *Desire*®
Published by Silhouette Books
America's Publisher of Contemporary Romance

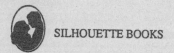 SILHOUETTE BOOKS

ISBN 0-373-05926-4

IMPULSE

This edition published by arrangement with Harlequin Enterprises B.V.

® and TM are trademarks of Harlequin Enterprises B.V., used under license. Trademarks indicated with ® are registered in the United States Patent and Trademark Office, the Canadian Trade Marks Office and in other countries.

Printed in U.S.A.

Books by Lass Small

LASS SMALL

finds living on this planet at this time a fascinating experience. People are amazing. She thinks that to be a teller of tales of people, places and things is absolutely marvelous.

To
Elsie MacLean
friend and sage
with my love

One

Speaking long-distance from Winter Haven, Florida, Mrs. Abbott assured her daughter in Atlanta, Georgia, "Well, Amy, you're perfectly welcome to come home right now, but why not stay where you are for another day or two? With the rain, you'd either be trapped here in the house, or you'd have to go somewhere else. Unless, of course, being twenty-four years old and wearisomely mature, you've become tolerant of Mitzie and Peck?"

"How do you stand them?" Amy Abbott Allen inquired with genuine curiosity.

"As you know, I'm very grateful Peck saved Bill's life all those years ago in Vietnam. I must add—however—the 'saving' is being told with increasing drama each year. I honestly believe Peck tripped at the crucial moment, but then you know how unbearably logical I can be?"

"I have seen hints of it." Humor laced Amy's droll words.

"Don't try to ingratiate yourself to me with flattery. I cannot hint the Peckerels away. You know that. And they are such a refreshing change for your father. He needs Peck like some people need an occasional dose of Laurel and Hardy."

"Peck is chatty, but he's tall and thin, so he must be Laurel?"

"Yes, and Mitzie is Hardy har-har-har."

Amy laughed with those sounds. "And what purpose does Mitzie serve?"

"I especially appreciate Mitzie's visits. Bill looks at me in awe for simply days after we've been with the Peckerels."

"I can't begrudge you that, Mom. Instead of staying here, I think I'll go to Saint Petersburg Beach." She sighed dramatically into the phone mouthpiece. "I'll sulk there until you finally get rid of the Peckerels."

"Be careful of the prowling beasts." Her mother's voice became gentle. "The wolves are always after little girls like you."

"Little? Mother, you fantasize. You know I take after Daddy." While Mrs. Allen was five feet two inches, Amy was five feet seven, and her father was six feet four. Amy declared, "I'm a woman."

"I…" But Cynthia Allen had hesitated too long, so she said airily, "Never mind, I'll tell you when I see you."

"Let me guess. You've found the perfect husband for me."

Cynthia chided, "Now, Amy, why would you say something like that?"

"I've known you all my life."

"It's been a delightful acquaintance, my love. I'm sure the Peckerels can't stay more than another few days. We haven't been too lively."

"You're very sweet to Daddy."

"I like him."

So on that early March day, Amy Abbott Allen drove her packed car from Atlanta down to Saint Pete Beach on the west coast of Florida. She drove under the portico at the Trade Winds, exited her car and went into the glassed lobby as the rainy evening came down.

On the lobby tree, the flamboyant parrots were tolerant of the attention they were getting from some of those in the laughing, milling group of well-dressed young adults to be registered.

As Amy waited her turn, she noticed most of the people in the lobby knew one another. They were having a teasing, greeting time, exchanging gibes and laughter.

That's when she saw him.

He was somewhat ahead of her in the casual line for the desk. He was one of that special, friendly group. Her first thought was: There's a man Dad would like.

Then she looked at him for herself, and a strange flicker went through her body before it concentrated in the bottom of her stomach.

He was big. Almost as big as her father. He was probably thirty. His suit perfectly fit his marvelous body. His hair was very dark, so his eyebrows were, too, and that explained his black eyelashes. His lower lip was full and his jaw looked stubborn. His lazy smile was being wasted on an obnoxiously beautiful redhead who flirted with him.

Any woman would flirt with him. Amy realized that right away. A woman could become quite silly in attracting him. She could be quite like a bitch wolf trying to impress the dominant male wolf. It always embarrassed Amy to see women be so obvious.

He didn't seem to mind the redhead's attentions as he stood so easily relaxed. He was probably that same way in the boardroom, relaxed and in control, but God help the careless employee.

He'd slay with one rapier glance, and he'd say, "Find it!" in a soft voice. And if that person made a second mistake, he'd...uh-h-h...he'd help the incompetent one to relocate. Amy scoffed that she could know all that about a man she'd only glimpsed across the crowded lobby of a beach hotel.

But that was exactly how he would be. She'd bet on it. It would be interesting to meet him...just to see if she was right. That was all. She wasn't going to *do* anything about him. She was only—curious. There were a lot of men who wore facades of authority, but they were actually hollow men.

When it came to pressure, they lacked the judgment, the background of information or the skill of business. She'd seen a lot of men, having traveled with her father in his business.

It was her father who had carefully guided her to know people and how to judge them.

Amy glanced over at— What would his name be? What name would such a man possess? He hadn't yet looked at her. That was unusual.

Men generally saw her in their first assessing sweep of a room, and she would meet interested eyes every time she glanced up. She had never deliberately invited such interest.

There in the lobby other men looked at her and talked for her benefit, ready to include her in their conversation. But *he* didn't even notice her.

He didn't need to look around. Women migrated to him like iron filings to an irresistible magnet. They had crowded him so that he was no longer in the line ahead of her but off to one side.

Amy thought such interest, from her, in a disinterested man was astonishing and, to distract herself from him, she began to listen to the group. How open they were! How careless with names and plans.

Privileged people don't care who hears their idle chatter. They rarely consider the other people who are around or listening.

Apparently the group was there for the redhead's wedding. The bride was talking solely to the formidable man. Amy wondered how her groom felt about his bride flirting with such a man.

Or was he the bridegroom?

The bride's name was readily available, since everyone was teasing her. She was Sally. And quickly, as Amy listened, *his* name was Chas, the diminutive of Charles.

Amy agreed with that choice of nickname. He wasn't a Charlie, although the redhead did call him Charlie in such a sassy way she must be privileged. How privileged? Amy's eyes narrowed on the redhead.

Then Amy thought, what business was it of hers? Well, at least Sally wasn't marrying Chas. The groom's name was Tad. Why the feeling of relief in her because the groom was not Chas?

"Any of Trilby's bunch coming?" One of the group inquired of Sally.

"Who knows? I couldn't find many and even they are all out of touch with one another. Trilby had ten children, all girls, and they married and scattered. With all the name changes, they've been hard to find. What we've found of the next generation, they were all girls, too!"

Some man's voice offered, "Our bunch came down fairly intact. Male, of course."

That male comment caused protests among the females and some teasing male laughter over the indignant female exclamations.

Since Amy was an only daughter, she was curious how Chas reacted to the thought of having only female offspring. She swiveled her head to see his reaction, but she even had to shift in order to look farther.

He was almost directly behind her! When had he moved? But she couldn't see his face since he was turned away, talking to someone else. Not the redhead.

He had a great voice. It was low and rumbled. Even so, it sounded as if he lightened it so that it wasn't too strong. It was still a commanding sound.

Amy's imagination could see him on a battlefield shouting for his men to rally. And they would.

Now where did an idea like that come from? How ridiculous! Perhaps she was intrigued because he didn't notice her.

When next he spoke, it was almost in her ear, and goose bumps flooded her body's surface. The sensation was so peculiar that she was distracted from the lobby banter among the wedding guests.

She was so distracted that she moved to the desk and just stood there. The efficient couple behind the desk smiled at her and inquired, "Do you have a reservation?"

"Yes. Amy Aaabbott." A couple of extra *A*'s in there, since she'd almost said Allen. She was handed the reservation card and signed it.

Being her notable father's daughter, she had begun to register as Amy Abbott, using her middle name. Her family agreed such action would be wise. Especially since she now traveled alone in this day and age. Who knew how strained and strange minds worked in revenge?

As she signed the card, she was aware Chas's breath stirred her hair. He was facing her way. Probably impatient with her dawdling? She was being as quick as she could. Efficiently she inquired, "Was the fridge stocked?"

"Yes, it was, Miss Abbott."

"Thanks." She smiled back as she accepted the card, which took the place of a key. She declined an escort and was directed to the complex map, which she studied. There was a huddle of buildings named and explained. One was an indoor, heated pool. She located her third-floor suite.

Amy then went out to the parking lot and moved her car to the guest lot. She took out her weekender and made her way through the hotel complex. There she walked to the deck elevator for the six-floored north wing.

In the elevator, she was again with some of the wedding party. As Amy looked out of the back, glass wall of the elevator, she heard one of the women ask a man of their group, "Is Matt coming?"

"Oh, yes. He's still trying to convince Connie to live with him."

"They're cousins," a woman commented.

The male's voice was lazy in his reply, "Only third, no problem. But Matt doesn't want to *marry* her, he just wants to get her out of his system."

"Connie's smart to hold out."

The male chuckled low in his throat. "I'm not sure she does, she just won't live with him."

Amy wondered how did the chatterers know she wasn't from a gossip magazine. They weren't even aware of her. At least the women weren't. To them, Amy could have been a knob on the panel. The doors opened on the third level, and only Amy exited.

From the elevator, she turned left. The access walk on the floor above served as a roof, so her walkway wasn't completely wet. She looked down on the second floor sun deck which, in turn, overlooked the courts for basketball, handball and tennis.

Through the well-placed palms, she could see the putting course and shuffleboard. Beyond was the bricked chessboard in the quadrangle formed by the buildings of the complex.

She went to Room 334 and put her sandpiper-marked card into the top of the lock. The lock's light turned green. Amy removed the card and opened the door. But instead of entering, she hesitated.

Why should she feel this odd excitement? Apprehension? It was as if she was about to cross not only that threshold but an additional one. Prickles went up her spine. Amy shivered as if with fear, or thrills, took that step and entered her suite.

Nothing happened.

She dropped her weekender on one bed and walked down the connecting bath-hall and through her living room with its kitchen bar. The wall was glass, and so were the double doors. She opened the sliding door, which gave access to her balcony.

She stood in the doorway, breathing deeply of the rain-wet, salt-scented air. To her left was the Gulf, the beach and the prerequisite palms. Then she looked down at the man-made waterways plotted around contrived islands and used for the foot-peddled paddleboats.

In the evening's darkness, Amy stood on her balcony in the dark, looking out on the calm scene. She was a little lonely. In just the last few weeks she'd begun to understand single men hunting companionship. Traveling alone was boring.

After being inside all day in meetings, there was the urge to do something physical in the evenings, to run, swim, anything that was different.

However, being a woman alone in such circumstances, in public accommodations, left her open to be approached. In all that time she'd met about every variety of male God could devise, and they were no big deal.

But traveling with her father had kept the wolves at bay.

Amy had served as a "side man" to her father during the summers, then full time in the two years since college. In that time, she had been listening silently and learning. She had been traveling for his political campaign advisory company for almost four months now on her own. It had been a revealing experience.

Her dad used her as a trusted representative. It was interesting work, but it would have been better if she was a man.

Men reacted to her not as Bill Allen's representative, but as a young female. Their reactions ranged from indulgence, to tolerance for Bill Allen's daughter, to genuine attraction, to lechery. But mostly they had trouble taking her seriously.

Where a man could have started at a basic level of acceptance, Amy had to work to reach up to that zero and *then* had to work hard for the men to even listen to her.

Her father told her, "It's good experience," and *he* ruffled her hair. He then grinned at her and said, "In another fifty years, they'll listen to you and take you very seriously with genuine respect. By then you won't be the sable-haired blue-eyed killer you are now."

She'd fingercombed her hair back into place and given the disgruntled reply, "I'll have it before then." Her father didn't realize his hair-ruffling was very like other male reaction to her. She was aware, but she could tolerate it from him since he was her father.

However, the next time she'd gone to have her hair cut, she'd told Peter to give her a hairstyle that would allow her father to ruffle it without destroying anything calculated.

Peter had groused a sympathetic, "Men!" He then spent almost forty minutes studying her head before he cut her hair in the matter of about twenty minutes in a neat, shake-right swirl.

Peter believed in style not fad, and he said, "You're lucky you can wear your hair any way you choose and forget it. You have enough hair, your head shape is good and your features are well placed. Ears can be a bore. Yours aren't bad." From Peter that was accolades only to her luck. He had meant nothing personal.

Below Amy's balcony, down on the pedestrian walkway, a group of wedding guests strolled along in the misty evening, laughing. Even from two floors up, Amy could clearly hear, "But who else will come?"

"Who knows? It'll be interesting to see."

How carelessly those elegantly, casually clothed people chatted. Anyone listening closely could intrude and pretend to be one of them.

Being oblivious to listeners was the way with any specialty group whether it was business, politics, travelers or, as in this case, monied people.

It never occurred to them they were overheard and someone could carefully listen. Look at the information she'd gleaned just in the lobby, the elevator and just now. They didn't actually know who all would be there at the wedding of Sally and Tad.

Even Amy, who had no ulterior motives, could go to any of them and say, "Well, hello! I'm a descendant of your Aunt..." Was it Tilly? No, not Tilly. It had been Trilby. "I'm your long lost cousin, Amy Abbott!"

She could say that quite easily. They didn't know all of their relations. Even those they knew weren't in touch with the others. She could fake being related.

And they would accept her. After a certain strata in life, people were no longer snobbish. They would include her quite nicely, for a time, just for the novelty if for no other reason.

All Amy had to do was take advantage of their careless tongues. She could do it. And if she did...she

could meet Chas! Ah, yes. Did Chas know he was a
carrot to her goatish...uh...ewe-ish desires?

If she did pretend to be related to them, it *would*
give her the opportunity to find out what kind of man
he really was. She would learn if he was solid or hollow. She could do it as a test of her father's school-
ing. An independent study. Test her skill of
summation. What a neat cover-up for lust.

Lust? She? Of course not! It was simply...
curiosity.

However, it would be interesting to have an affair
with him. To have him look at *her* with that sinfully
lazy smile. To have him bend his head down to hear
her and watch her mouth as she spoke. To be the object of his attention.

She might be able to do that, too, with complete
immunity. Not only could Amy Abbott Allen invade
their celebration, but she could contrive to have an
affair with the dominant male wolf.

They were all strangers, she wasn't native around
there. She could very easily perpetrate such a mas-
querade...and get away with it.

She did pause. Again. It was another threshold.
Was it the one she'd sensed as she'd entered the suite?

She was contemplating a very rash thing here.
Strange behavior for the puritan Amy Abbott Allen.
It was one thing to fake an acquaintance and invade a
private gathering just to see if she could, but it was
another thing entirely for a woman of her upbringing
to even think about plotting an affair.

An affair with a stranger she'd only glimpsed in a
hotel lobby? Insane! She'd been working too hard.
She was alone too much. Her male contacts called it
burnout or nerves or relaxation or distraction or al-

most any other word. She'd always sneered and called the affairs predatory usage.

Could it be she was no better than any prowling male? Women did do this sort of thing. Amy knew they did, but she'd always thought they were a different kind of woman.

Perhaps Amy's interest now was only because she'd never before seen a man she wanted.

Amy did want to try for him.

With the decision, she spent a long time listening to a wild, shocked debate inside her head—all of which she realized she'd heard before! Had she only been thwarted from seduction by her conscience? Was she a victim of Victorian morals?

She was not! While not quite past this one, she was a Twenty-first Century Woman!

She could live like any man. She could take her pleasures as she found them and enjoy the freedom of choice. She could.

She could stand on her back legs and howl just like any others of the wolf pack. She could go right ahead and have an affair, right there, with Chas...if she could entice him.

What if he wasn't interested? Well, there were others in the party. She could... No. She could look them over again, but she hadn't seen any of the others who'd rated a third glance.

It was to Chas that her eyes had clung. It was *he* whose body spoke to hers. She wanted him.

And of course, she had the advantage of being unknown. She could vanish into the night, like a highwaym—highwaywoman.

* * *

Lochinvar had carried off the bride. Amy would be a female Lochinvar. One who carried off a man from a wedding celebration. It was an omen.

He'd be something to try to carry off since he was so big. And she only wanted the affair. It would be an affair of mystery for she would vanish. Would he pine for her? Search?

Her mind made up all sorts of tales of his search. He'd stand on the outer edges of her life, she would at last recognize him and she would be kind.

No, that would never do. When she left, it would be finished. She couldn't have old lovers turn up here and there. That would make her life too cluttered.

The affair would stay an interlude of enchantment. And he would never know who she really was.

Of course, once she met him, there was the chance that she might not be interested. He could well be hollow. But the opportunity was there for her to find out if he was a solid man.

She didn't have to languish through the days of simply catching glimpses of him around the hotel. She could get to know him, and she could judge whether or not she wanted to know him . . . better.

Wasn't that the word men used? "I'd like to know you...better." All she had to do would be to enter their group, *ta-dah!* and reveal herself as a long-lost cousin!

Having that distraction from boredom, the affair would entertain her. She had to have something to do until Peck and Mitzie left her parents' house. She could read up on the campaign of Harry Albert Habbison, who was running for a State Senator's job in Illinois.

H.A.H. seemed so relaxed and easy, but he was about the shrewdest hayseed she'd ever met. He was going to use the State Senator's position to campaign statewide, and he'd then become a U.S. Senator or he'd have scalps.

Amy was curious what her father would do with her notes in working up a rough on Harry's campaign. Harry had a good chance of winning his district. And in a sampling in the state, people didn't yet know of him.

That was good. If they had no opinion of the unknown, there was nothing to counteract.

In Illinois, the Republicans had always ruled the state while the Democrats held Chicago. But that was changing. Could a Republican hayseed make it? Harry thought so. How would her dad advise on that, and what would be his comments on her notes? It would be interesting.

Amy's father was considered one of the country's most brilliant campaign advisors. A lot of gimmicks were attributed to him. The handwritten notes whose ink actually smeared. The shirtsleeves and loosened tie with suit coat carried over one shoulder with the left fingers holding it—leaving the right hand free to shake any hand.

The coat over the shoulder was attributed to Sinatra's long-ago album cover, as Mr. Allen pointed out. Although, before then, his candidates had used it—for a time.

By now the folksy, shirtsleeved bit had been so overused, and used so awkwardly and with such calculation, that no Allen-advised candidate touched such a cliché.

Any Allen campaign pattern was so quickly copied that he allowed others to take credit for them, because by then he'd gone on to better ideas. The senior Allen didn't like to be coupled with ideas that were past their time. The only thing he pointed to—with clients—was who had used him and how many had won.

So, naturally, there was the question as to how many of those who won had beaten better men? Whose side to take was faced with every potential client.

The preliminaries for the decision was Amy's job. It turned on who was the client, his reputation and how he reacted to her.

She probed as to what sort of people were around the candidate and what were his goals.

There had been potential clients who'd been turned down who had won. And there were good men Allen had accepted as clients who'd lost. No one won them all.

So what would her dad do with Harry A. Habbison? Something ought to be done with that double *H*. Her father might shun such a gimmick. Honest And Honest? Double *H* for double Honor?

The man was honorable. She'd stake her judgment on that one, but he was peculiarly unpalatable. However, the H.A.H. might be used by the opposition as the derisive sound, *hah!* Maybe they shouldn't draw attention to his initials.

What was Chas's full name? Now there was a man who would tempt any woman to vote for him. Chas, the dominant male wolf.

A woman always wants the best man around. And there was the warrior in Chas which would inspire men to believe in him. Ah, to have Chas for a candidate client. All they would have to do would be to put him on television and ask him to say his name and what he wanted.

Amy really didn't care what he wanted. She wanted him. She wanted to talk to him, and have him look at her, smile at her, to reach out, put his hand on her nape and draw her to him. Yes.

It was getting quite cool with her balcony door open. Why would she stand there, in the cool wet darkness, dreaming about a man who hadn't even looked at her?

He was probably a loyal husband with six kids. Any wife of his would willingly have six kids for that man. She...well, no, she wasn't having his children. She simply wanted an affair, if he was single.

She was going to try. Tomorrow she would contrive to meet Sally and introduce herself as a long-lost cousin. And after that, it would only be a matter of time before she met Chas. The impulse was a little heady, and she felt a strong recklessness. It would be an adventure.

Two

Amy had gone to bed so early that she wakened at a completely uncivilized time on Thursday. The morning's gray sky was still dripping. With the balcony door open, the air smelled fresh and cool like San Francisco's fog.

Instead of using one of the beds in the bedroom, Amy had opened out the sleeper sofa in the living room and slept there, snug and warm under a fleecy blanket.

She stretched and stretched and yawned before she lay peacefully in an unusual indulgence. She'd heard there were actually people who wakened before they got up. She could get used to it.

Her empty stomach indicated it was hungry. She could easily eat there in her suite, from her stocked supplies. However, the time factor made utilization of The Relative Plan rather urgent.

It would be wiser to go down to one of the dining rooms for breakfast in order to begin her deception. Did they serve this early? Would any of the wedding party even be up?

Amy sat up and swung her legs off the sofa bed, then stood and stretched as she enjoyed just doing that. Going down the suite's hall into the bedroom, she looked at her wardrobe. She'd have to get some more things from her car.

She flicked through the few things hanging there and pulled out a shockingly expensive jogging suit. She'd bought it because the color matched her blue eyes exactly, and it beat utilitarian gray bulk all hollow.

Amy surveyed herself. She did not look like a serious athlete.

Her headband was an old one from her father. It bore the label McMahon, for the ex-quarterback of the Chicago Bears. She picked up a purple-hooded sweat jacket, put her door card in the back pocket of her pants and went down to the breakfast room.

Quite a few people were there! What were all these people doing up at such an ungodly hour?

There was a hum of conversation in the room, and the waiters moved around. There was the clink of plates and rustle of people.

Then Amy realized most of the diners were wedding guests. In her quick scan, she didn't see Chas. But she did see those present were dressed in a wide range of casual sports clothing, and her impulsive sports buy wasn't beyond reason.

She chose a seat within earshot of Sally, the redheaded bride-to-be, in order to pick up on any men-

tion of their Aunt...was it Tilly? No, it was Trilby.
Their "relative in common."

Amy noted that Sally wore a deliciously baggy old
gray utilitarian sweat suit. Sally could wear a barrel
and still be a knockout. Amy was glad Sally was getting married. Chas's cousin or not, Amy wanted Sally
out of the way.

Looking over the menu, Amy threw caution to the
wind and ordered a monster breakfast. Eggs with an
S, pancakes, trout, bacon, strawberries and tea. And
she ate it as she listened only to the table next to hers.

The bride said, "The dresses haven't arrived."

The woman with Sally soothed her. "They'll get
here. Don't panic."

"The wedding is *Saturday!* The day after *tomorrow!* I don't want to get married in this sweat suit."

"You have that green dress."

"I used to wear it with Frank."

"Well? So?"

"Every time I wear that dress, I think of Frank, and
even you will have to admit I can't marry Tad while
I'm thinking about Frank."

"Why don't you give it to the League's Second
Chance Boutique?"

"It looks terrific on me." Sally's voice was deliberately mild in her acceptance of looking great.

"I have to agree to that. Did I ever tell you I once
stole it? But when I put it on, it looked like a dishrag
on me, so I put it back."

"The color is wrong for you. You have a great figure."

"It was too tight."

"So that's when it happened! Do you know *I* had to
mend that seam?"

"Old Simmy would have been proud of you!" Sally's companion exclaimed as she laughed. Then she asked, "Where is Tad?"

"He and Chas went on a soggy jog."

"Chas is probably having to tell Tad what marriage means."

"Tad knows."

The other woman chuckled in a very amused way.

Then Sally said, "There she is!" And from the corner of her eyes, Amy saw Sally straighten and lift a hand up just above her head. She rose in welcome as another woman, in a traveling suit, came to the table to be hugged. Then she was greeted by others of the wedding guests before she was settled at Sally's table.

"Matt will be glad you got here. He was sweating it. He wasn't sure you'd come. I told him you'd have to be here to witness me actually getting married."

Matt? Amy tried to remember what she'd heard about a Matt. Someone had said something about a Matt last night. Moving in with...

"Connie, do you care for him at all?"

Connie. Matt wanted to live with Connie, who apparently was reluctant. And Amy waited like a soap-opera fan to see what Connie would say.

Instead of answering, Connie asked, "Have the dresses arrived?"

Impatiently, Sally told her, "No! Your asking that means you're not going to tell me about Matt."

Quite primly Connie's voice replied, "You're not involved."

In a teasing way of old friends and cousins, Sally pushed it, "I ought to get some sort of reply. Here we got up at this *ghastly* hour to welcome you! And anyway, you're my maid of honor. You owe me."

"I did come." Connie was still formal and withdrawing. "Did you find any of Trilby's bunch?"

"Who would dream any of Trilby Winsome's winsome offspring could be so elusive. No one can find anything about five of the daughters. Faith, Hope, Charity, Prudence and Ellen. They've vanished into..."

With opportunity knocking, Amy interrupted from her table to say, "I beg your pardon. I couldn't help overhearing. This is a very strange coincidence, but my grandmother was Charity Winsome...Abbott."

For an endless minute, the three women at the other table stared at Amy, then Sally smiled and questioned, "Really? Well, hello, cousin!" And the other two laughed and echoed the greeting.

Amy smiled, and with applaudable restraint, she returned to her meal. She was aware the other three women exchanged questioning looks and minute shrugs. But after that they talked more softly among themselves, more privately.

Having finished eating, Amy signed her bill. She rose from her chair, smiled at the other women, who smiled back, and left the dining room. She had planted the seed. What an interesting thing to see if it would germinate. She felt she had handled it perfectly.

As she left the morning room, Chas and...Tad, the bridegroom, came inside. Chas looked right through Amy. He didn't even see her.

But as she went through it, she caught her arm on the door and stumbled as she looked back. She saw that he'd turned to watch her. She looked away immediately.

He wasn't so indifferent to her, after all. Hah! If Chas only knew it, the preliminaries to their affair were progressing splendidly.

On her way through the quadrangle toward the beach, Amy went by the glass windows outside the morning room. She looked into the room from the slitted corners of her eyes.

She saw Tad was leaning over Sally, as Chas was moving Amy's vacated table next to Sally's, while Connie and Sally were talking and indicating Amy to the men. Amy walked on. With her last discreet glance, she could see both of the men had looked up through the windows at her.

Walking away, she smiled inside, with an odd lick in her lower stomach. If Chas only knew what she had planned for him! Ah, yes. Would he tremble in his Nikes? He had probably had affairs with every woman who caught his attention.

That would be the trick! She would have to catch his attention. Then she would lure him into bed the way men did women. She would use him for her entertainment.

But for now, she would have to wait.

The wedding party bunch were good-looking people. It would be nice to really be kin to them. Being an only child, Amy had always longed for a big family. Would they approach her?

She would be discreetly available if one of them did. They were so curious about Trilby's children that Amy doubted if they could resist at least questioning her.

Since they knew nothing of that branch of their family, Amy could be quite easy about her replies. It's too hard to remember lies. While keeping her own identity secret, she would tell the truth as nearly as possible.

With that premise to entertain her, Amy went out on the beach and walked leisurely south, down toward the pink palace. She found some sand dollars and was disgusted with herself for collecting two handfuls of shells. She had *boxes* of shells!

Collecting shells was like drinking beer. There is more beer in the world than anyone can drink so no one should try to drink it all.

There were also more creatures in the sea making shells than she could ever collect, and she ought to quit picking them up. Even as she thought of that, she stooped over and picked up another one! But it was another perfect one.

Trudging in the spent waves, Amy wondered what color were his eyes? Blue? With his hair that dark, they would probably be brown. He was beautiful. Formidable. She nervously licked her lips. Maybe she ought to just move to another hotel and forget this whole thing.

The plan was reckless. Were men this strained in the planning of a seduction? Or did they just take women as they came along without any qualms at all?

If men could manage, then she could handle it. Out of bed, anything men could do, she could do. Equality. By George, she wouldn't be a quitter. She'd see the seduction through. She'd planted the seed of curiosity and it ought to grow.

By the time she arrived at the pink palace, sitting flauntingly on the beach south of the Trade Winds, Amy was experiencing a fresh feeling of determination. She turned back to retrace her steps along the beach.

She ruthlessly shoved her shells into her clean purple jacket's pockets, washed the sand from her hands in the swirl of the waves, getting her sneakers wet. She squished along, her head bent to the mist. The lumps of shells in her pockets bumped in soft clinks against her thighs.

Besides Amy, there were other idiots walking the beach. However sparsely, there were others out. Therefore when a man's muscular, gray sweat-panted legs came along in front of her, she moved to her right, but he matched her move and his Nikes stopped.

She looked up and...it was Chas! My God. His eyes were green! Very green. She simply stared.

"Hello, Amy Abbott. Or should I say 'Cousin'?"

He was so cool. So adult. He was not one that any idiot would trick. This was the man she was going to trick? Uh huh. This one. She questioned, "Cousin?"

"You told Sally, Elaine and Connie that you're one of Trilby's issue."

"No. I said my grandmother's name was Charity Winsome. I only know that. I have no idea what Charity's mother's name was." She watched as he smiled faintly. He knew she lied? She contrived to look honest and straightened her spine. A straight spine is always honest.

"Your eyes are blue."

She nodded, admitting that.

His husky, deep voice said softly, "With your being a third cousin, that makes us kissing cousins."

Her eyes became enormous over the idea of being kissing cousins with Chas. She was so bemused by it that she watched his head block out the rainy sky as he leaned forward and kissed her simpleton mouth. She simply allowed the opportunity to pass without doing anything!

Good grief! She stood there as if she was fourteen again and it was her first non-party kiss, for God's sake. He lifted his head and smiled at her; and he had creases at the corners of his eyes that were enormously attractive. She took an unsteady breath as a part of her mind said: Hmm, this might be very, very nice!

"If your Charity is part of our family, her mother was Trilby Cougar Winsome. Trilby was my great-great-aunt. Apparently—from the stories—she was a pistol. Unpredictable. Are you that way, too?"

He knew! "No." Her voice was thin. He couldn't possibly know.

"I'm Charles Cougar. My friends call me Chas. So do cousins, Cousin Amy."

"Cougar? Are you kin to Indiana's John Cougar Mellencamp?"

"Cougar isn't John Mellencamp's real name. When he first started, his record company named him John Cougar. Our name comes down three hundred years from Billy Cougar. He was a hunter in the Appalachian system. He wore a cougar's skin on his back with the cat's head on his head. That's how he got his name.

"We know he was a Brit. An Englishman. But we have no idea if he was a younger son come here to the New World to make his way, or if he was deported." He grinned at her. "But he was a hunter, a trader and an organizer."

"Yes." She was still not working on all cylinders. She was distracted by the fact that she was trying to figure out a way to get another chance at a cousinly kiss. "How did you know my name?"

"I was in back of you when you registered."

"Oh." She wasn't being too swift at conversational allure. If she planned to entice this man, she needed to be a great deal more sparkling and interesting. She inquired politely, "Did your wife come with you?"

He couldn't prevent a laugh. He controlled it quickly, but he had laughed. He replied nicely, "I'm not married, are you?"

She solemnly shook her head, her eyes never leaving his. Why was he so amused?

"Let's go back to the hotel," he suggested. "It's getting a little wet out here." He took her arm, and they went on back.

The shells bumped against her thighs as she lengthened her stride to keep up. She felt like a fool. She ought to tell him right now she was a sham. Yes. She took a breath and said, "Ah . . ."

"You will come to the wedding? It's going to be in those rooms off the lobby. With the fountains? Have you seen them? If it's still raining, they'll cover the roof so it'll be warm enough. You will come?"

She nodded, still very serious, but she realized just how fragile this opportunity was. She needed to take hold and use it. No man would be tongue-tied and silent. He'd flirt a little and smile. Did men have to work this hard?

She stretched her mouth incredibly and managed a small grin. Then the whole ridiculous situation hit her funny bone, and she laughed. She boldly took his hand and pushed back her hood enough so that she could look up at him, striding along beside her, and she actually swung his hand a little as she laughed again.

He grinned back and his big, warm hand enclosed her small, cold, wet one. He was playing along! Did preying men feel this sense of exhilaration? But as she watched his smile, her eyes lifted to his, and his eyes were guarded. He was suspicious of her.

Did she look like a predator? A predator like some of the men who had pursued her? There are men who women instantly recognize as dangerous so they can avoid them. Had her intent changed her into something else? Had it changed her from the safe, businesslikc woman into a huntress? Did her very pores smell of danger to men, telling them to beware?

And Amy considered that the men who looked predatory had probably once looked bland and safe. Criminals eventually had a look about them that was hard and scary. It could well be that women changed, too, as their life-style was changed, and . . .

Such thinking was all completely idiotic. She'd been working too hard. Her imagination had never taken control this way, before now. Of course she'd never before deliberately set out to seduce a man.

"Where is your home?" Chas asked.

She blinked once to come back to the reality of being with Chas. "Home? A suitcase. I travel."

"Oh? And what makes Amy run?"

"I'm in research. Polls." That wasn't too far from the truth.

"That must be interesting. What do you ask?"

"Depends on what we're researching."

"House to house?" he inquired.

"That, too, depends on what we're researching."

"Phone banks? Boiler-room surveys?"

"Even that sometimes." Her reply was also true.

"What is your firm?"

"Freelance." She had to smile at his effort to pin her down. He probably would never fully know how adroit she had been in replying. Too bad. He would appreciate the game.

Now, how did she know he'd appreciate her intrusive game? If he knew she was being tricky, it would more than likely make him mad. Men didn't like being fooled.

But what *he* liked didn't matter. It was what she liked or wanted that mattered. And she could well decide to want Charles Cougar. Cougar. Men were supposed to walk like cats. He walked like a hunter of cats.

They separated to change into dry clothing and met in the glassed corner of her floor's discreet nook of chairs and tables. He rose as she came around the corner to him, and he suggested, "Why don't we go up on sixth and meet the others?"

"Others? There're more of you?"

"Oh, yes. And not all of us could come. So there are even more of your newfound family for you to meet another time."

He said "another time" so casually, as if there could be a future for them. "How many of you are there?"

"They all have kids so fast we ought to be called rabbits instead of cougars. I don't know what the latest count could be. We'll see if anyone on sixth knows. Come on. They're dying to talk to you. And of course you'll go to the wedding. Will you need a gown?"

She shook her head. He went on, "Some of the pools are heated. We might swim later, before supper. We're on our own tonight. Do you play chess?" He gestured to the waist-high chess pieces on the clever brick board sitting idle in the soft rain.

Again she shook her head.

"Well, how about putting? When the rain stops, we can do that?"

She nodded. She'd been a runner up in a golf competition at their club during the summer she was twenty. She could handle golf.

He was telling her, "Tomorrow night's the bachelor's dinner in the main dining room. Everybody goes to the dinner. That'll be fun. You'll learn a lot about the family skeletons there. Tad's family are nice people. You'll have a good time."

They were inviting the fox right into the chicken house? She smiled in a foxy way. It would be an experience. What a story this would make when she next saw her best friend Elsie! Elsie would say, "You did *what?* I don't believe it."

But Elsie knew Amy didn't have enough imagination to make up this impulsive madness. Elsie would have to believe it. Or…would she ever tell Elsie? She'd have to wait and see how it all turned out.

They went up to the sixth floor where the wing's whole series of suites were opened together, taken over by the Cougar Clan. Chas and Amy went from suite to suite and were welcomed with laughter and chatter. Amy kept saying, "I may not be any kin at all!" The truth can be said so that one is safely misunderstood and accepted. How strange that was.

"If you aren't, we'll adopt you," Matt announced, and Connie gave Amy a rather cool look.

So Matt was a flirt? Connie was jealous? Would Connie finally move in with Matt just to keep him? Ah, What a tangled web we weave when first we practice to deceive! How unknowingly we influence other lives. Would her bold intrusion cause Connie to do something rash? Would she do something she wouldn't ordinarily have done?

The Cougars accepted Amy. That unquestioning acceptance made her a little uncomfortable. And Chas stayed close. He would say, "I'll tell her about it and see to it she gets there." And that easily, Chas established them as a pair.

Did women fall into men's laps this readily? Did men simply decide who they wanted and then just wait for it to happen? It was amazing! No wonder men were womenizers. There was no sweat to it at all.

Chas, the catch of the entire clan, was hers! And it was he who'd paired them off. After this, she should be able to get him into bed in two days at least. By Saturday. Right on schedule.

The clan all had lunch together, still talking. The clouds broke, the sun came out, the sand absorbed the rain and dried on top.

The wedding dresses arrived, and some of the women went to try on the dresses. Tad was teased about whether or not he had the ring or had ordered the flowers. He was tolerant. For Amy, it was like really being a member of a large clan. It was nice.

After lunch, Chas pulled Amy to her feet and said they were leaving. They made their goodbyes and went back out into the bright afternoon. They strolled through the marvelous myriad latticed walkways, around and over and throughout the complex, through the open and sometimes on hidden, secret stairs.

As they chatted quite casually, Chas said, "Since you're a cousin, I wonder if you'd volunteer to help out the family. My cou—*our* cousin Robert and his family, with four kids, haven't a reservation."

Chas explained in an aside, "The eldest didn't have chicken pox after all. If you wouldn't mind, I could bunk with you, and they could have my place." Chas's face was bland and logical.

He elaborated, "If we can't double up enough, they'll have to stay at another hotel, and they'll miss half of the fun. I can give them my suite, but I don't want to move away from the hotel, either. How about letting me sleep on your living room couch?"

Now that was fast! In the space of a couple of hours, she'd not only been accepted as a cousin into their clan, but now Chas was using "family connections" to move into her suite. Good grief!

Amy's mouth fell open and she gasped. Then as her blue eyes hit his very green, very steady *watching* eyes, she thought: In this situation, a man would jump at the chance! Really? This wasn't... She hadn't planned... This was really very fast. She said, "Uh..."

"We're cousins," he reminded her mildly. "It would be okay."

"Well... Uh..."

"Some problem?"

"No, no. I just..." But she couldn't think *what* she just. He was going to move into her suite—just like *that!* If he did move in, it would make the maximum opportunity syndrome very maximum, all right.

She couldn't get her conscience-stricken vocal chords to do anything. But with some concentration she got her head to go up and down—once each way.

He accepted that lame movement as agreement and said, "Robert and Jean will be so glad. This way, in my suite, they can close the door on the kids and have the living room sofa bed all to themselves and not have all of them jammed together into one room. That's restrictive for couples with kids." He added that thoughtfully.

He still held her hand as they walked along. She'd met him about—what—five hours ago? And here they were, walking along, holding hands. He'd already kissed her within the first minute, and now he was going to move into her suite.

Her seduction was really going along very quickly. She ought to be jubilant with things working out so well. But instead, she felt rather as if she'd stepped on a merry-go-round and was having a little trouble balancing to its speed as it carried her around quite madly.

He said with quick efficiency, "I'll just run upstairs and nab Robert to tell him the good news, and I'll be down to your suite with my things in about five minutes. If we go by your place, you can let me have your lock card and wait for me there."

So that's what Amy found herself doing. They took the garage elevator up to the third floor and walked around the deck to her place. She unlocked her door, handed him the card and he left.

Bemused, she wandered on through the bedroom, down the bath hall and stood in the living room. She was feeling as if she'd just now stepped off that merry-go-round and was unsure which direction she was supposed to go.

It did occur to her then that surely some of Chas's clansmen had an extra bed. But if she was intent on seducing Chas, this certainly presented a remarkable opportunity. Another handy opportunity.

She had snatched the first one, and now here she was, that much closer to her goal. Any man would be dancing and grinning and exuberant!

Her prize was at hand! And there she stood, wide-eyed and astonished. It would begin. So easily! Actually, it had started. How would it end?

Her deck door opened, and Chas busily wheeled in a double-ended hanger luggage cart. He efficiently emptied it as she simply stood there and watched, with her arms hanging from her shoulders.

He put things in the bath, in the bedroom closet and in the vacant bottom drawer. He added things to the refrigerator. He was moving in.

He smiled, gorgeously. "We'll have to go down to re-register me with you. I'll split the bill. No long-distance calls without my okay. Know anyone in China? India?"

Very seriously, she shook her head.

"Peru?" He was being funny and enjoying it.

But he was also laying down rules. She understood that. He was. It was her suite, and he was laying down the rules.

Well, that was good. There had to be some ground rules if they were going to share the suite. He in the living room, and she in the bedroom.

Three

Chas and Amy went back up to the sixth floor to find out if there were any specific clan plans, which they might want to consider. They found a rather organized chaos. Some of the kin were planning to fish in the Gulf the next morning, and some were driving over to Disney World.

And as they moved around, they encountered another cousin, Kenneth Cougar, who was promising Sally he would be back the next night for the bachelor's party.

"Leaving us, Ken?" Chas asked.

"Just a quick trip." Ken named the city. "I have to see a rising kingpin, Martin Durwood, and this is a good opportunity."

"Martin Durwood?" Amy found herself asking.

"Yes. Know him?"

To leave the festivities, the meeting with Martin Durwood would have to be important to Ken, her new "cousin." Amy replied, "Yes." Then she inquired carefully, "Do you know him?"

"No. Not really." Ken gave her a steady, measuring glance.

She cautioned, "Be careful."

Both men focused on Amy almost as if they had opened second eyelids, their gazes were so intent and piercing. Ken asked, "Why?"

Chas asked, "How do you know Martin Durwood?"

Tellingly, she replied to Chas first, "A . . . survey." She frowned a little at Ken. "What I have is privileged. Just be careful."

"You don't like him."

"There's a saying. Let's see. Yes, 'If you shake hands with him, count your fingers.'"

"Oh?" said Ken. He lifted his head a little, intensely alert. Then he lowered it as he pushed up his lower lip and nodded several very small movements.

Chas then told Ken, "Listen to her."

And Ken smiled at Amy. "Thanks, cousin. I'll let you know tomorrow night what I find out." He gave Amy a rather formal nod with a warm smile. As he left, Ken clapped Chas on his shoulder and quite cheerfully said, "You lucky bastard."

And for some reason, Chas laughed.

It was just as Elsie always said: Men are different.

It was amazing for Amy to be absorbed into the wider group of strange people and accepted by them as one of them, without any effort on her part. Again she understood it was Chas who had maneuvered the phenomenon. So it was their trust in Chas that was involved. He had accepted her, therefore the rest did.

The most startling thing was how freely they spoke of the most intimate things. As Amy had thought once before, in listening to them in the elevator, they were fortunate she wasn't from a gossip magazine.

As sometimes happens in a crowd, a quiet fell, and one conversation suddenly became general. A cousin was saying, "Well, after that they couldn't allow her to be buried in the family plot. She's off to one side, at the edge of the cemetery."

"Who?" someone asked.

Another cousin hastened to assure them, "She wasn't an *in-law*. That would account for several who never made the family plot, but Letty was a Cougar. Letty Cougar Milstone Wiggins LaCross Bernard. Those are the ones she married."

"It wasn't her interest in *men* that shocked everyone," a female cousin said in a fact-keeping way.

"No. You're right," agreed another cousin. "The Cougars have always had a strong attraction for the opposite sex."

That caused a good, indulgent chuckle among those cousins and siblings in the crowded suite.

But then the subject was changed, the different areas of the completely opened suite complexes led to more separate conversations.

Amy never did find out what Letty had done to be forbidden the family burial plot. Think of being shunned even in death! She wondered if Letty wouldn't have wanted to be planted in another place entirely.

Before long, the cousins and siblings drifted outside. Especially the northerners wanted to be outside in the lovely March day. They shed jackets in the sunshine to walk and stroll the beach and select shells or play some of the games available.

Amy had never been anywhere in all her life where she suddenly knew so many people. It was marvelous fun to hear shouts of encouragement when she and Chas were in one of the paddleboats. Or to be watched by others as they used the putting course. And the critical observation with snide remarks when they were a part of a tennis foursome.

Men can feel competitive in sports with women, but Chas didn't. She could never match his physical strength, but he paced himself so that their game was fun, and she could show off. He was an unusual man.

Only the Yankees joined her and Chas to swim. True Southerners know full well only Yankees and idiots swim outside that early in the year. Chas was so warm-blooded he could probably break ice and dunk himself without realizing the cold.

How marvelous it would be to sleep with a man like that. And she would soon know what it was like. By Saturday. The day after tomorrow.

Although Amy was dark haired, she had a redhead's complexion. Her skin burned and didn't ever tan, so she used sunscreen, and she didn't sunbathe. Therefore, she seldom swam outside.

So it wasn't remarkable that she swam at an indoor club and her suit was a practice Speedo. It was perfectly comfortable. Although it was cream colored, it was cut high in the neck, front *and* back, and it fit down over her hips for swimming comfort.

It was, indeed, comfortable. However, as feminine attire, it didn't begin to compare with the other suits on display.

Chas smiled at her as she reluctantly took off her toweling robe. Then he gasped, "My God, you could be naked! It's like a second skin." His eyes glinted and his smile widened.

She blushed in pleasure. But for a modest woman, why should she like it that she looked almost naked to him? She reasoned she liked his saying that because he might not be too reluctant to submit, if it pleased him to look at her.

It certainly pleased her to look at him. She had to do it in quick glances because she had to resist the need to stare at him. He was something! He was so beautifully male. No one would mistake him for anything else. A no-waist-wedge. Nicely hairy. Muscles. His bathing shorts were like those of all males.

She was getting a little excited about him. Some unusual licks of feelings coiled and uncoiled deep inside her body. She had to swallow and blink.

She could swim quite nicely and she didn't mind getting wet, so they played recklessly. She tried vigorously to drown him. He handled her without any effort at all. He chuckled. He had a great laugh.

His hands were a little careless but not groping. He let her take a breath before he pulled her down in the magic waters, and he kissed her very uncousinly.

She *might* be able to get him in twenty-four hours! That would be some sort of record, she was sure of it. Men weren't the only ones who had their wily way. So did Amy Abbott Allen, the man-izer.

They said men notched their bedposts. How would she keep track? A pencil mark on her closet wall. A perfect solution. That would be discreet.

Then only she would know the full extent of her conquests. Her reputation would remain intact, and her mother wouldn't start searching for a Presbyterian convent.

Now why wouldn't people be as tolerant of a woman, who was a man-izer, as they were indulgent and titillated by a man who was always after women? Prejudice. Everyone should fight prejudice.

It rather pleased Amy to think she was taking up the Women's Cause in seducing Chas. It gave a nice tone of unselfishness to her indulgence.

She sneaked a peek at him. How brave of her to seduce him for womankind. She laughed.

He looked up and grinned back. "What's funny?"

She replied, "The day. The sun. Your ineptness in swimming?"

He took her to the bottom of the pool again. And again he kissed her. As they surfaced, and she pushed back her black hair, her blue eyes were almost hidden by her water-spiked lashes. She said, "See? You're on the bottom of the pool all the time. You don't know how to stay on the surface!"

She almost made it to the edge of the pool before he caught her. She laughed and gasped for breath, knowing what he'd do—again—but instead he held her across his arms and moved her about the pool in the most charmingly peaceful way.

He was powerful. His muscles roiled as he used them in handling her. His movements were so effortless. Seemingly effortless.

It no longer pricked her conscience when his family called her "cousin." How quickly she had adjusted to being a part of them. From her lazy pool bed, with Chas her movement and buoyancy, Amy saw Connie and Matt walking along the latticed path as it wound near the pool.

They were speaking intently, unaware of their surroundings. Connie wouldn't look at Matt, although he took quick, serious glances at her. Amy thought they were quarreling.

If Connie didn't want to move in with Matt, what was their problem? Then Matt started to leave Connie, and she put out her hand and stopped him. How strange. If Connie didn't want Matt, why did she stop him? Was she holding out for marriage?

Maybe Connie should just . . . have an affair, Amy decided, as she would with Chas. And she smiled at Chas, who smiled back in a very smug way. Amy wondered what he'd think when she made her move.

Very kindly she put her hand up and smoothed his wet hair back from his forehead, and he made a purring sound. Somehow that startled her, but then she remembered Chas was a Cougar.

They probably made all sorts of jokes about being feline. Feline sounded too feminine. He was a lion. Mountain lion, cougar, puma. A loner. Dangerous.

And there was a sensual lick going through her body again? It was a little scary.

They got out of the pool, and she put on her robe. But Chas wrapped her head in a towel and put another around her shoulders. He put on his own robe and roughed his hair with another towel. "Let's go back to our room." He said it so naturally!

There was no reason to get into a quake over the idea of it. She ought to be giving him alluring glances and inviting smiles. She was a little cold in the March air. She'd wait until she'd showered, washed her hair and was dressed. Then she would begin.

What if he turned her down flat? There wasn't the time to wait for clues of reciprocating attraction. It was very like men traveling. No time for the preliminaries, just, "How about it?"

She found she had some qualms over the abruptness of her past refusals. She could have been kinder. She'd always been so insulted, she'd been rude. What if Chas said to her, "Get lost, dummy!" as she'd said that first time. Or her exasperated, "Good God!" not even a week ago.

Men couldn't score every time. They were bound to meet some Amy Abbott Allens here and there. It must be dreadful for men to be turned down. With all this sweat of preparation, if it was her lot to be the man, and Chas as a woman *did* agree, she'd probably shrivel up with nerves and wouldn't be able to do anything! Why did men keep trying?

Chas said, "I don't want you to chill. You get in the shower first. Do you need your back scrubbed?" His inquiry was polite.

She blurted an, "Oh, no!" and closed the bath door. She scrubbed her hair. She'd never shared a hotel room with anyone. She never had to sort out shampoo or razors or anything like that. How strangely intimate to see Chas's things mingled with hers.

She blow-dried her hair before she realized she hadn't brought in her clothes. There was a knock on the door and she jerked on the wet swim robe, clutching it to her before she asked, "Yes?"

"I have a choice of things for you to wear."

She opened the door and laughed. He leaned forward and smiled as he said, "You look charming."

In something of a fluster, she chose a long, silky, T-shirt type pullover that came to her calves. It was a splashy blue and lovely. She again closed the bath door, replaced the robe with the gown and put on enough makeup to simply look healthy. She tidied the bath and walked out, saying, "It's all yours."

He was still smiling as he looked down her body. "Very nice."

"Am I supposed to help you find something to wear?" How bold she sounded!

He wondered, did she know what sort of reply he could give to that? "I have slacks and a shirt. Do they meet with your approval?"

"Well, I'm not sure. What else do you have?" She smiled, but she bit her lower lip. She needed some practice. She felt so blatant!

He led her into the bedroom, her bedroom, and opened her closet to reveal his clothes hanging intimately next to hers. "The tux is for the wedding, but there's plenty of time to have it freshened and pressed."

"A bit formal," she decided.

"Blue suit? Shirt and tie?"

"Well, I'm not quite that formal."

"Slacks and shirt?" He grinned.

"Perfect."

He laughed and rumpled her hair, and she laughed an excessively delighted little female laugh that star-

tled her. She'd never in all her life laughed in that as-
inine way!

He said, "There's a bunch going across the street to
the Oyster Bar for supper. Or we can go for shrimp
and oysters and then come back here and order a
pizza. It's a neat bar. Shall we go for a while? There's
a dance floor. Wear stout shoes." And he went to the
shower.

She took advantage of his greater height and wore
heels.

The Oyster Bar was a two-story building and the bar
was upstairs. The entrance was two story and painted
a very dark blue with antique farm tools set high on
shelves. The wooden stair was sturdy and there was a
strong handrail.

Around the bar were tractor seats, and the room was
large and painted the same dark blue. There were tables for four, with single, low lights above each of the
booths around the wall, and there was a bandstand.

There was a large video screen with rock and roll,
country-western and sixties songs everyone knew.
They all sang along. No one could notice the volunteer singalong, because the bar was a loud, party
place. The oysters were served in ice-filled tin trays.
They were delicious.

And Chas danced with Amy.

He danced perfectly. So perfectly that other cousins came and demanded he dance with them.

Chas smiled kindly and said, "How about later?"
Or he said, "Not now."

After the cousins had tried, strange women felt free
to come up and invite Chas to dance.

Amy was surprised at the feelings the women's conduct aroused in her. She was possessive. But again he kindly turned the women down. Not "No" but "Perhaps later." He never did dance with anyone but Amy.

It was heaven to dance with him. He knew exactly what he was doing, so he could do it effortlessly. Amy didn't really care if they danced or not, although she did appreciate his skill. She would have been just as thrilled to simply be held against him. He held her perfectly. He felt so good against her body. His arms were enclosing, and his breath was sweet.

He twirled her and dipped, he did the Peabody, he could dance any step. He made her look terrific. It was his skill in leading her, she only followed his directions as his hands moved to guide her.

As he brought her to him after a dip and moved forward to her backward steps, in male aggression, she laughed—secure in his arms—as she looked up and asked, "What did you do to learn to dance so well? Are you a closet gigolo?"

"My mother was adamant. She said, 'All your life you will be in circumstances where you can dance. It beats sitting and drinking and listening to drunks. Learn to dance.'"

Chas looked down into Amy's face as he hesitated deliberately in his step, holding her. Then he added, "I'm glad mother is right again. I'm glad she hounded me into learning. I despised it at first. But I enjoy moving to the music with you. I like moving with you." His voice was husky and low as he held her tightly to him on the crowded floor in the noisy room.

His comment was very close to flirting. There had to be something she could reply that would hint that she was interested in him. She should have paid more attention to the men who came on to her.

She tried to remember what they had said and how they had handled themselves. She'd never been interested enough to really listen and respond. She lacked tactics.

Were there books? When you got to *The Joy of Sex* you were pretty far along. There had to be some intermediate maneuvers before you actually had a man in bed.

Chas held her close to him there on the dance floor and said in that smoky voice of his, "I'm hungry."

"Shall we go back for the pizza now?"

He smiled, so amused about something, and replied, "Why not?"

They took their leave discreetly, exited the bar, recrossed the four-lane busy road at the light and went back to their suite. He didn't rush her at all. He was skilled in working with strange women.

They sat on their balcony, sipping wine, as they discussed the complex, the weather, the night and the coming wedding. They went on to current news, and he fetched the bottle of wine.

With the end of their second glass, he suggested ordering the pizza. She was agreeable. He inquired, "Surely you're not an anchovy devotee?"

She apologized, "Yes."

"My God. They set up the entire anchovy distribution just in the hope of pleasing you?"

She returned placidly, "I'm worth it."

His lashes came down to conceal the fires that leapt in his eyes. "How do you justify making the entire rest of the world say, 'Everything but anchovies,' just so they're available for you?"

"I travel."

"And you know Martin Durwood."

"Only because of an inquiry I did." She found she didn't want to lie. There was nothing against being misleading, but she couldn't lie outright to Chas.

"In your surveys and inquiries, do you choose designated places?"

"Pretty much."

"Who do you work for?"

"Several . . . organizations."

"Amy Abbott. . ." Did he deliberately pause? "Are you the Pilgrim the name implies?"

"Ah, yes. An innocent." That was the truth! "Actually, the Pilgrims would have been strong women who had to have spines of steel to have gone onto the *Mayflower* and survived here. We've been around that long in this country."

"Women in general, yes, but you mean your own family?"

"Oh, yes."

"Mine, too. Besides Billy Cougar, or whatever his name really was, we've been here all along." He watched her.

"If this is Show and Tell, tell me about Charles Cougar. What do you do?"

"The family is involved in many things. I happen to be in manufacturing. It's a thankless job. Not the romantic sort to entrance a lady. It deals in facts and figures, unions and contracts, deadlines and overruns on occasion."

"What would you prefer to do?"

"Manufacturing," he replied simply. "I find it a challenge. I have a great sense of supplying things people need. I love it. I only meant it's rarely something for social conversation.''

"You have no desire to be a pirate?'' That had been what she'd expected him to say, and she could have believed his doing that much more quickly than for him to be contentedly bogged down in the nitty-gritty of manufacturing, for God's sake!

"A *pirate!*'' He raised his unruly eyebrows. "I'm a law-abiding man with no tolerance for cheats. Ah, here's the pizza. Sit still.''

He moved too smoothly for a law-abiding man. He moved like a dangerous man. He was like one who knew how to get from here to there, see everything in between and not be seen himself.

He said he was law abiding and had no tolerance for cheats. Cheats like Amy Abbott Allen who had insinuated herself into the Cougar clan? If he found her out, before she vanished into oblivion, how angry would he be? What would he say?

He returned to hand her one of the kitchen towels instead of a paper one that would blow away. They sat companionably, sharing the pizza and wine.

He was relaxed and his conversation was amusing. He looked around, but he only rarely looked at her.

When he did look at her, Amy felt it to her core. Her body reacted to him so strongly that she began to doubt if she wasn't quite stupid to become involved even so casually with Charles Cougar.

He tidied up the debris, and Amy began to think how awkward it would be to say she would be going to bed. It was the first time in her entire twenty-four years she'd been in this particular situation, alone with a strange man.

He was extremely, potently male. What if she said, "Come on to bed," just like that? She looked at him in speculation.

He glanced up at her as if her look commanded his response. Then he handed her the cable guide. "I think there's a film at ten that I've been wanting to see. *Take It Easy with Me!*"

She was jolted by his words. He *knew* what she intended for him? He knew she planned to seduce him and he wanted her to be kind? "What?" she asked in some embarrassment.

"Have you seen it? I understand it's above the average. Shall we give it a try?"

He wanted her to watch TV? That was a shock! He must feel quite safe with her. She found his feeling safe was a little annoying. She felt a bit petulant but opened up the guide and there it was listed: *Take It Easy with Me!* It came on in ten minutes.

He put some brandy on the end table before he busily opened out the sofa bed! Then she realized he was telling her in a very ordinary way, "Why don't you get the other pillows from the bedroom? We'll watch in perfect comfort." He stopped and gave her a look. "You do want to watch it, don't you?"

"Sure." She thoughtfully went in to the bedroom and returned with four additional pillows. What a scene for a seduction! Pillows, TV, bed opened out. Yeah.

Could his seduction be *tonight?* Her nerves shimmered. She couldn't possibly seduce him tonight.

She wasn't ready mentally. She *could* get in some serious kissing, and see if he responded. She'd hate to have him bent back over her arm and have him say, "No," to her. She'd die.

"Take off your shoes before you get into my bed."

Get into my bed? That's what she was doing; she was getting into his bed. Just to be comfortable in order to watch the movie. *Take It Easy with Me!*

She was filmed with sweat as she shivered a little. This was a nerve-rending business. By Saturday, when she actually seduced him, she was going to be a complete wreck.

"Shall we leave the sliding door open? It makes it cool and cozy. I'll get one of the blankets." Without comment he extinguished the lights behind the kitchen bar, leaving only one lamp on at the end of the sofa bed.

Efficiently he made the nest. He turned on the TV and the preliminaries had begun. Amy slipped off her heels and crawled onto his bed. His bed. She had slept there just last night. Tonight it was his bed. She was on his bed.

"Comfortable?" He unbuckled his belt, causing her to gasp, but he simply pulled it from the pant loops and pitched it over onto a chair. "Got any belts you want to remove?" he inquired chattily.

"No." It was a quick reply.

He removed his shoes and settled into the nest, taking up an unusual amount of space. Amy had never in her life shared a bed with anyone. He was big. He crowded her.

"Have a sip of brandy." He watched the screen as the movie came on ... a man and a woman in a hot, hungry embrace, their hands prowling, their mouths moving as if to consume.

Amy watched, fascinated, her cheeks heating, her body reacting very strangely.

Chas said, "Ahhhh," in soft appreciation.

His sound electrified her body. She would like to have Chas kiss her in exactly that way and make that same sound. It was disturbing to watch two other people doing it while she sat tensely in a pillow nest, with a man like Chas, on his bed.

Something interrupted the clinch on the screen, but Amy wasn't sure what. She was so aware, so concentrated on her body's reaction to being there, on his bed, with Chas, that she was distracted from the story.

Chas took her glass from her inadequate fingers and lifted it to her mouth. His eyelashes almost covered his green eyes as he watched her obediently take a sip. He smiled as if she'd done well. Then he put the glass off to the side table, as the liquid fire burned down her gullet . . . and it . . . ssprreeaad.

He turned back to her and kissed the brandy on her lips. He sipped several little kisses from her mouth, then he shifted. His mouth pushed her head back and his hands moved on her, laying her backward into the pillows as the kiss then became a very serious one as he leaned over her.

The excitations that rioted inside her body went completely berserk! She gasped, and he kissed her just like that kiss on the screen had been. Hungry. Intense. The seduction of Chas could begin now! All she had to do was make her move!

Four

To seduce Chas that night would place his seduction two days ahead of schedule! A rather shockingly sudden move. Amy was a very organized woman and to rashly disrupt the sequence of events was disquieting.

Her thought brakings were distracted by Chas, who reached to click off the remaining light. Then he kissed her again. His breathing was unsubtle and somewhat erratic.

He gently began rubbing his face slowly all over hers in the most erotic manner. His hot breath was quick as his mouth sweetly took small, burning kisses along the way.

He was so like a cougar that she expected to hear him purr, but his sounds were human and very male, relishing sounds.

Amy was sure a twenty-four-hour acquaintance and seduction had to be something of a record even for a man. And so, lying there in that nest of pillows on his bed, flat on her back with the cougar bent over her, trapping here there . . . Amy made her move.

She slid one hand around his back, but the other hand she *deliberately* lifted to his nape, to cup his head with her hand.

There. The die was cast. Now he knew her intentions—blatant and bold. She wanted him. She would have him. Then she even turned her body toward his!

She had expected some reaction from him. A gasp of surprise. Perhaps a hesitation as he realized what she'd done.

He didn't gasp or jerk in shock. He moved his hot mouth under her ear and breathed his hot breath there, nibbling and rubbing his evening whiskers gently on that tender skin. And his right hand moved from her stomach to her rib cage and then up to cover and squeeze her breast.

How many women had he made love with that such a bold signal from her hadn't startled him? But his hand moved, kneading, pushing, squeezing. Then that hand went down to her hip and around to her bottom and spread there as he pulled her strongly against his body.

How quickly he'd become aroused! How astonishing. And marvelous sensations swirled around in a lazy turn from her ribs down to her core.

He probably wouldn't say no. He would be willing. She could become bolder.

She put both hands to his head and slid her fingers into his thick black hair. Then she sought his mouth in order to be kissed. She wasn't exactly sure how to go on from there.

He didn't seem to worry about it. He kissed her with remarkable skill and began pulling up her skirt. That caused flurries of almost panic inside her chest and her breaths became quite erratic.

Still kissing her, he managed to lift her enough to get the skirt up around her middle and push her panties down to her knees. Then he touched the inside of her thigh, up high.

It was just a good thing he was half lying on her or she might have jumped right through the wall. She did gasp and jerk, and her body trembled so that Chas slowed down and petted her as he made soothing sounds, and his kisses became like gentle rain. Scalding rain.

With the last shreds of coherent thought, she gasped, "I'm not on the pill."

His slow voice breathed in her ear, "I'll take care of you." Then his mouth moved down to nip her nipple beneath that silken cloth before he opened his mouth over it and nuzzled and suckled the flowering bud hidden there.

Her knees bent up, and she writhed, and her panties around her knees were hampering so she kicked them off.

He laughed low in his chest as he rode the motion, and the next thing she knew he had the dress off over her head and she was stark naked.

Suddenly her feet were freezing. Cold feet? It was *true!* "I'm naked." She was astounded that was so, so she felt the need to mention it.

"And I'm not. Well, I can fix that."

He lifted away from her and knelt up on the bed. He was going to put her dress back on her? She wasn't sure she wanted that. She rather liked being there like that, with him, in his bed.

In spite of the fact that she was in the dark, she covered herself with her hands. And she could feel she was blushing fiery red, but she wasn't about to stop her seduction. She still wanted him.

In the flickering light of the TV, Chas tore off his shirt and flung it aside. Then he stood on the floor, to get rid of his trousers and underwear.

Amy got to watch Chas put on a condom. He appeared to know how to do that quite well. He'd probably practiced.

He returned to the bed and crouched there, looking at her from head to toe in the same flickering light from the television. He reached one hand to her and watched her body as he smoothed his hand over her and up to her face.

It was so intimate. She was so aware that she was female to his male. His voice was somewhat hoarse as he said, "Beautiful. God, Amy, you are simply breathtaking."

Her lungs labored and she had to breathe through her mouth. She would have figured her distress was embarrassment at being naked...except that all her nerve ends were shimmering in excitement. Her knees rubbed minutely and she licked her lips. She wanted him against her.

She reached a hand to touch...his arm. It was textured with hair. She was excited by the touch. It was so intimate.

His arm. Yes.

But he loomed there, watching her, and his hand cupped her face as he leaned and kissed her almost chastely. "Are you sure?"

That she wanted him? How maddening! "Of course!" Why did he think she was seducing him? She was almost irritated with his hesitation. Did he plan to back out on her? She half rose and said, "If you don't want—"

Making his voice lighter, he quickly replied in a very soothing way, "Amy. Come to me. Stand up."

He helped her off the bed and drew her to him. He deliberately rubbed his hairy chest against her bare breasts, then he slowly pulled her hesitating body against the length of him. She was surprised by him. Holding herself away from him, she asked, "Will I hurt you?"

His voice was a tad ragged but very earnest as he assured her, "Oh, no."

So she allowed herself to be pressed against him. From chest to thighs, she was against the hard maleness of him. She felt his hard hairy chest, the pressure of his iron-hard arms and his muscular, hair-textured thighs.

Her stomach was against the hot shaft of his bulky sex. The size of him was intimidating.

"It will never fit." She stated that flatly and felt bitterly disappointed.

His smothered rumble of laughter was so amused. He hugged her, moving his hands on her back in a soothing way, and he assured her, "Everything will be fine. No problem."

She wasn't convinced. She put her head back and looked up at him. "The statues never show anything like—well, they are all much smaller. I don't believe this is going to work."

"Really, honey, it'll be all right."

With some surprise, she asked, "You've done this before?"

"Uh..."

"No, I shouldn't have asked. These sort of things shouldn't get too familiar and—"

Cautiously, he asked, "What—sort of things?"

As a woman of the world, she replied in an instructing manner, "Affairs. Since they are only brief encounters, there shouldn't be any exchange of past details. I... this is my first time."

He didn't say anything.

She laughed a little. "I've surprised you, haven't I? Well, I have been out of the mainstream, and I just never tried it. So when I saw you, and being here and all, I thought it might be a good time to see what it was like."

His breaths were harsh, but his hands had turned so gentle. He kissed her temple and then held her with exquisite tenderness. "Why me?"

Quite frankly she replied, "I've been in a man's world for years. Traveling with my father..." Whoops, she almost gave it away. She went on in a stilted, formal manner, "I've been rather closely chaperoned. However, I have heard things, and several times men have approached me. I never wanted to before. I thought you might be willing." She had tugged him back down onto the bed. "I'm getting cold."

His voice blurry, he was earnest. "We can't have that!" He tucked her in beside his heat and held her. "Let's take it easy for a day or two and see how things go."

Her slight gasp caught his ear.

"Have I been so inept?" she asked sadly. "Was my approach all wrong?"

"You've driven me out of my mind." That was certainly true. He hadn't noticed her "approach" because he'd been too concentrated on approaching her. Hadn't she realized how he'd moved in on her both physically and actually? She *was* naïve! She was probably a virgin, or was she immeasurably clever? Could a practiced woman be this innocent? She was at least twenty-two? "How old are you?"

"What does that have to do with sex?"

"You're over eighteen?" he asked in some alarm.

"Just because I'm not very good at seducing a man doesn't mean I'm a child!" she exclaimed quite indignantly. "I am twenty-four."

"Guessing women's ages is a tricky thing to do. I met a twelve-year-old not long ago who looked twenty-five. As soon as she opened her mouth, you knew that was a very high guess, but she still could have passed for eighteen—and she was *twelve!* Women baffle me." He lay back and put his hands behind his head.

She turned so she was curled against the warmth of his side. "Men are a complete unknown to me. I know the mental side of business and men, but the physical is beyond me. I have no brothers, no sisters, either, but I've never before seen a naked man. You are quite beautifully made."

"Thank you. I return the compliment. You bend my mind out of shape and you do strange things to my body, too, if you've noticed. I'm just a tad obvious."

"Could I . . . touch you? Are you warm? Is it like ears? Cold?"

"Right now my ears are quite warm, and you have my permission to do whatever you like, if I may have an exchange of privileges?"

"Well, you already touched me, you do remember that?"

"Oh, yes. If you want to touch me in my seminatural state, you'd better be quick. You're getting me excited again."

"Am I really? How nice of you to say so!"

"Don't you realize how you affect men?"

"I've never tried before now."

His lips parted and it was much too late for her to examine a latent male.

"Could I turn on the light?"

"We'll have to close the drapes. Someone might look over here."

"Okay." She hopped out of bed and pulled the drapes across with the attached handles. "Now." She got back onto bed and knelt beside him. "May I?"

He reached and turned on the light. He laughed a little in an awkward way, amused, titillated and just a bit embarrassed.

That charmed her. She leaned and kissed his mouth. Then she sat back on her hip and looked at him. "How interesting." She touched him, and he reacted to her. She was fascinated. "You are amazing."

"I'm a man."

"Oh, yes."

"Amy..."

She turned serious eyes to his green ones. "It will fit?"

"Yes. I promise it'll be all right. I'm not at all unusual."

She made the decision. "If you really don't mind, I should like to try it."

"How did you live twenty-four years and stay so innocent?"

"I don't believe I'm that unusual, either. There are as many women like me as there are the others. Especially with the diseases, there are a lot of women who don't believe in free sex, or they've never had the opportunity, or they choose not to be distracted, and there are those who just aren't interested."

"But you're interested?"

Seriously she regarded him. She replied softly, "With you."

"Are you real? Did anyone put you up to this? Am I being tricked?"

Her eyes flew back to his. Tricked! He suspected? "I simply want an affair." Her voice was genuinely earnest. Then she added the rider, "No strings."

He reached a hand out to her nape and asked softly, "No strings?"

She shook her head.

He pulled her down to him, his mouth opening. She leaned down willingly, her breasts brushing against his chest, and she gave him her lips. He said, "Open your mouth."

She did, and he gave her the most amazingly sensuous kiss she had ever imagined. His tongue met hers and unbelievable feelings shivered in her stomach and breasts.

She moved until she lay on him. Her breasts were exquisitely sensitive to the texture of his hairy chest. One of her hands moved on his chest, then, on its own, that hand moved down his body to touch him, to caress, to tease him. He gasped a groan and made such savoring sounds that she laughed in her throat.

"You tease," he growled low and wickedly amused. "Laugh, will you?" He moved her effortlessly, turning her onto her back. He looked at her, lying there, as if she was a feast. Then he set himself to enjoy it all.

If she could have gotten out from under him, she would have climbed the wall. She said, "No wonder..." And she said, "I understand..." And she said, "Oh..." a good many times. And she whispered, "Chas..." even more times.

He did fit, as he had promised. And after she adjusted to his invasion, the feel of him was a marvelous thing. She cried in little gasps, her emotions were so high.

So were his, for he'd never had a virgin before, and he was very tender and sweet to her.

Their bodies filmed with sweat as he carefully led her through the paths of love, as he patiently took her with him, to the heightening plateaus, and to that ultimate peak to paradise.

She gasped in astonishment and clutched at him in the sweet, tumultuous madness that rocked them to their cores. It was the ultimate burst of sensation, and they fell slowly back onto their bed, leaving them limp and spent.

Eventually she murmured, "No wonder men hunt women. No wonder women are learning to do that, too."

"This was special." The old hand instructed the new girl. He lifted to his elbows and looked down at her in the lamp's light.

In her innocence, she asked, "Isn't it always like that?"

"It's always nice. But it's seldom like that. That was amazing."

"Wow. And I made it the first time." She grinned up at him.

"It might be only with me." He felt an odd possessiveness rising in him.

She laughed in a murmur of *M*'s. Then she told him, "You are terrific."

"You're amazing. I can't believe this happened."

Just then, she heard the swelling sound from the TV and looked at the screen to see: The End! "The movie's over! We've been all this time!"

"Yes."

She murmured vaguely, "I wonder how it ended."

"Fabulously." He put a hand to her head and leaned to kiss her cheek.

She smiled gently. "I'm glad you were my first."

"Amy..."

She confessed openly, "I'm going to put a mark inside my closet to keep track. You'll be my first mark. I don't want to notch my bedpost. Mother would think I was cutting new teeth."

She burst into laughter. "I guess I am at that! This was wonderful! Thank you." She reached up her arms and hugged him to her, then she gave him a rather sassy, free and easy, smacking kiss.

"Amy..." His deep voice had taken on a cautioning tone.

"Is that too bold? I probably should be shy? I can't! This is absolutely the most marvelous thing I've ever done in my entire life!"

Still lying under him, she flung her arms out from her sides. "I feel like I'm in a candy shop and can't decide which kind to try next! I suppose I could just go out and tell men, 'Line up and I'll choose.'" She laughed over the picture of her doing such a crazy thing.

But Chas was appalled. He said, "Amy—" for about the fifth time. But he didn't know what he wanted to say after that. They'd just had a world-class sexual encounter with a shared climax! That came so rarely as to be remarkable, but he didn't know this woman under him.

How could he lock himself into a permanent relationship with a woman he'd just met? He said, "Amy . ." again. Then he kissed her, because he was going to move from her, and he wanted to do it nicely.

But she exuberantly wrapped her arms around him again and kissed him back.

His desire stirred.

That too seldom happened after so complete a release. She was remarkable.

She was as frisky as a pup, as delightful as one. She was maddening as a delicious woman, and again irresistible. And he made love to her again, but without taking them to completion.

They tumbled and laughed and teased and taunted. They coupled and parted. It was fun.

When they lay panting, resting, she said in a disgruntled way, "I've wasted a lot of time being so pure."

"No!" his voice was harsh when he'd planned only to be firm. "It's because you've behaved yourself that you have this delight. If you'd been sleeping around, by now it would all be stale and quite routine."

"Really?" With no knowledge of how gracefully sexual it was, she rolled over onto her stomach to prop her chin on her hand so that she could study him. "You seemed to have a good time and not find it all that stale and routine."

"I haven't had all that many experiences." He looked her straight in the eye, and he said, "Not all men are bed hoppers."

That made her curious. "Then how do you know what to do?"

"My parents. Books. My dad and mother must have a great relationship. They always told us kids that sex is one of life's gifts of responsibility."

She smiled. "My mother and dad really like each other. They knew each other a long time before they married. She was a virgin on their wedding night." Amy thought for a minute and added, "I don't think I'll get married. I like being in the business world. Taking a part in things. And now that I know I like sex, I'll be a man-izer."

"No." The word was quite positive and left no question as to its meaning.

"Well, this is a fine time for you to make a statement like that!" She laughed and ruffled *his* hair quite sassily.

His voice rumbled deeply as he replied, "I don't want you to become a careless woman. A tart."

Impishly she inquired, "Why didn't you say that when you found out you would be my first lover?"

"I'm not an iron man." He was serious.

She put her hand on him. "Not iron? Phooey. Steel?"

"Be careful," he warned. "I've never had a woman excite me the way you do. I could not put you from my mind. I wanted you."

"Before I made my move?" She was delighted. "You, too?"

"Yes." He was more solemn.

She saw that and said, "Don't go getting serious on me, Chas. This is an interlude. No more. You're being very nice about showing me the ropes... Uh—knowing the ropes. Do you suppose that saying came from sailing days?"

"What?" He was at sea.

"Showing someone 'the ropes.' I suppose that could be an old salt showing a new kid how to tie knots and haul lines? Are you an old salt?"

He ignored her conversational lure. He told her, "I'm going to climb on board and sail you into oblivion." And he did. With great skill he made her frantic for him, and her needing him—that badly—fired him to new heights, so that their coupling was exquisite and their satisfaction complete.

They sighed and smiled at each other, then he reached to turn off the light before he pulled her to him, arranged the blanket, turned off the TV, and they slept.

For the second morning, Amy was awake at dawn. It wasn't that she wakened rested and ready to get out of bed, it was that Chas was moving his hands on her, nuzzling his face against her, hungry again. She said, "You silly old salt. Go back to sleep!"

But he didn't. She turned away from him, plumped her pillow and settled down. But he moved close, curled into her, his mouth seeking, his new beard causing goose bumps on her as he whiskered her tender skin.

She chuckled. His voice rumbled in sounds that sent sensations skittering along her body.

He slid his hands over her uneven body and touched and stroked. He turned her to suckle and nip.

She wiggled and squeaked and laughed for a time, then she moved languidly tempting and joined in his sensual play until they made love again.

She stretched under him, and his green eyes watched her. "Will we do anything else today?"

He was positive. "No."

She grinned at him, then reached up and played with his ears and smoothed his eyebrows. "If I got into the pool, I'd drown. I couldn't move enough to stay afloat. How do married people survive?"

"I'm just trying to figure how I'll manage the energy to get dressed for the dinner tonight and attend the wedding tomorrow."

"Sally invited me to a hen party after the dinner tonight. Okay?"

It thrilled him that she had asked his permission. Was she aware that she had? "Don't be too long." Then, oddly, he added, "Be careful of yourself."

"Why?" She gave him a naughty look. How had she known to do that? She deliberately lowered her lashes and made the look wicked.

He grinned and shook his head. "You could turn into a dreadful tease."

"Not a tart?"

"No." He was serious again.

"If you will get off, I need to take a bath. I'm quite sticky."

"I'll bathe you." His voice cracked.

"Now *that* I can do by myself. I did need you to show me how to do sex, and I really appreciate it. I'll never forget you. But I can bathe myself."

"It could be fun to bathe you."

She sassed, "I might let you another time."

"When we have lots of time. Like now."

She protested. "I am absolutely starving!"

"Go bathe. I'll fix your breakfast."

"How do you know what I want to eat?"

"I saw your plates yesterday morning. You have the appetite of a stevedore!"

She shrugged as she grinned. "I won't ever get fat. Our family..."

"I'll see to it you get enough exercise."

She grinned. "I know. Swimming, golf..."

"Bed."

"That old exercise!" She sighed and let her arms collapse out on the bed.

In a gruff voice, he said, "I want you again."

She frowned sassily at him. "Are all men insatiable?"

"Only me with you."

"You are terrific." She pulled his head down to kiss him. "I'm a little sore."

"I suppose you would be. I've been greedy." He moved carefully from her. "But as with any exercise, you can adjust to this new variety."

She laughed again as she rose from the bed. Dragging the top sheet along to cover her front, she collected her dress and pulled it over her head. "You sound as if we're going to work into a routine."

"Aren't we?" He lay watching her.

"We can't get into a routine in just another couple of days."

"No," he agreed. "Not in a couple of days."

In the silken dress, she turned and gave him a thrilling view of her short, tumbled hair, her saucy face, her back and the curve of her breast as she looked at him, quite level eyed. "That's all there will be. I leave on Sunday."

He readily agreed, "Of course." But he smiled at her.

She went into the bathroom and turned on the water to fill the tub. Then she went to the very neglected bedroom and chose a pair of shorts, a pullover and underwear. She went back to the kitchen and asked, "Do you always cook naked?"

"I make it a point to get down to basics."

She nodded, accepting that. "Would you like to bathe first?"

"I'll shower during your first course."

She cautioned, "Don't get carried away. I only eat a normal woman's portion."

"Got it. Hash browns?"

"No."

"Hustle up."

She left him busily working and returned to the bath and stripped. She sprinkled some bath oil into the water and settled in blissfully, allowing the water to fill as full as it would. Then she turned it off to lie there, smiling with her eyes closed.

"A mermaid."

Her eyes popped open to see Chas standing there magnificently. She blushed and her hands flew to cover herself, but she smiled a little.

He squatted down, leaned over the tub, plunged his arms into the water to gather her close as he lifted her to him and kissed her.

"What is it about me in water that makes you want to drown me and kiss me?"

"You won't drown," he assured her gruffly. "I'll keep you safe. You need to get out. If you don't and I get into that tub with you, mermaid, we'll have to fix another breakfast. Yours is ready."

She sat up, then accepted his hand as she stood. "I'm absolutely starved!" She grabbed a concealing towel and discreetly began drying herself.

He helped, but he was selective where he dried. He commented as if in relief, "Well, at last I've found something to distract you from sex."

Her eyes became serious. "Chas. Do you feel as if I've...used you?"

Sadly, he declared, "My body's all that interests you."

"Well." She considered him carefully. "You do have marvelous eyelashes."

"How nice."

Concerned, she pressed. "Chas, I haven't hurt your feelings, have I?"

"I'll live." He turned away in a slumped posture. Still gorgeously nude. But he was a perfect model for the Defeated Warrior.

Amy frowned after him. Then she hurried into her clothes and tidied the bath as he brought his clothes in to have them ready for his shower.

By the counter bar in the kitchen-living room, her place was set at the table. There was cranberry juice. There was a covered dish with eggs and bacon. And toast was in a covered hot bowl. He had done an excellent job of it.

She ate with good appetite, but she squinted her eyes out over the complex.

Chas had opened the drapes and the sliding door onto a perfect day. Did he really know she had just picked him up to use him for sex?

While that was true, it would be a shame for him to feel as if he'd been a...sex object. She couldn't allow that.

Affairs might be more trouble than they were worth. She didn't want to hurt his feelings. But she was so grateful she'd found him.

She went over all the men who had seemed attractive to her in these last months, and she wondered if any one of them could have been as marvelous as Chas. Not one.

He was the epitome of all males. She couldn't imagine doing such an intimate thing with any other man she'd ever met. She'd been lucky he had come along at just the right time.

But... But... But how would she ever find a man to match him? Ahh, there was the rub. Was she allowed this taste of paradise because she would never have another?

Surely that wouldn't be so. Surely she would find others? If she never did, she was glad she had had him. It was worth it. He was worth all this effort. What a special man he was.

Dressed, he came to the table. His hair was still wet. He sat down across from her and smiled at her. "I like having breakfast with you."

"You know that I travel? I am very seldom at home. So seldom that I live with my parents on those rare off times."

"Where is that?"

"No exchange of information, remember?"

"I, too, travel. I thought our paths might cross on occasion."

"No, Chas. I could get used to you."

"Would that be so bad?"

"I'm not ready."

"I'll give you my card. If ever you change your mind, you would give me a call?"

She asked very seriously, "Would you want me, eleven men later?"

"An entire football team?" He expressed great shock.

But she nudged it. "You do understand me."

"I would have to see you, Amy. I think we should explore this magic between us. It's like nothing I've ever experienced. Is it us? The weather? A spell? Would it last? We hardly know each other's names, and look at this miracle. I want to keep in touch."

"It's only an interlude," she warned him. "Push, and we'll have to split now."

"You're a hard-nosed woman."

"See?" She smiled gently. "I'm not perfect."

"Close enough." He grinned at her. "Eat your breakfast. I have a car. I'll take you down the coast a way. I'll find you a memento so as you'll remember me."

"What?" she asked. Her eyes were gently on him. Memorizing him.

He replied casually, "I'll know when I see it." And he looked at Amy.

Five

During Friday, the rest of the Cougar clan began to arrive for the wedding. First came the young marrieds, then the couples with families and finally the rest of the senior members.

The influx was filtered with laughter and greetings and family talk with exclamations that bordered on rude. "So you're still wearing that?" "My God, Freddie, you're skinny as a rail!" "When's the funeral?" "Ah, Chas, are your parents here? No? Still in *China?* When did they go there?"

Amy heard that. It was a relief to her to know Chas's parents would not be there. She didn't know how she would react to their knowing their son was—uh—shacked up with a stranger who was claiming to be kin.

By then, the extended Cougars had begun to realize Amy wasn't a visitor, she was "one of Trilby's" offshoots. With their probing questions, it was about then that Amy began to understand about the Spanish Inquisition.

The questioning was intense. "So? One of the Trilby's?" That was said with a disbelieving stare.

One who lies always keeps to the simplest replies. She responded, "I'm not sure. My grandmother's name was Charity Winsome, but I have no idea about her mother's name." And Amy wished desperately that she'd never been tempted to begin this charade.

However, about that time she saw Chas across the room, and she couldn't regret his intimacy. Her first.

Another relative observed in a critical drawl, "You don't look like us."

Chas replied to that, "She has the Cougar dark hair."

"It's different," was the flat rejoinder. "Hers has a red glint, and ours is black."

"Connie's blond," Chas mentioned and he did try to keep his face somewhat serious. However, the lights in his eyes danced with his humor.

"Connie isn't a genuine Cougar," was one old lady's quite tart, dismissive reply.

An older man decided, "Let's claim Amy as one of us. As good-looking as she is, who cares? Come here, child, and give your old 'cousin' a kiss."

Amy did smile, but she pressed back against Chas, who intervened, "Now, now, Bart, remember all the older ladies are here and know you well. You need to behave yourself."

So while the younger ones had accepted Amy quite casually—although not with the enthusiasm of Bart—the older ones were suspicious. Amy avidly wished to God she'd never started the farce.

But if she hadn't, she wouldn't now be sharing a suite with her "cousin" Chas. So how could she regret her foolish, impulsive intrusion into the Cougar gathering?

On the hotel's sixth floor, there were pockets of busily visiting relatives, but there were always several who concentrated on Amy's background.

"Who are your parents?" they asked.

"The Aaabbotts." There were those extra *A*'s again. She had almost said Allen, her true last name.

Especially older people tend to pin facts down. One asked, "Where do you live?" A simple question for a simple reply. It was an easy question for almost anyone. Except Amy. How was she to respond with telling everything.

In her impulsive leap to an affair, Amy had never anticipated the grilling by Chas's family. It was obvious she would have to attend to the concoction of some sort of background. She hedged her reply, "Well ... Dad moves around."

"What does he do?" How routine that question is.

But Amy responded lamely, "Uh ... polls."

"You're not very chatty, are you?" was the critical, adult observation.

Again, Chas replied for her. Very kindly and openly, he told the quizzers, "That's the way pollsters talk. Haven't you ever been a victim of a pollster? They say, 'Answer yes or no—Have you quit beating your wife?'"

Chas waited for the usual groans that question always brought, then he went on quite loyally, "Pollsters all prefer one-word replies. It simplifies counting answers."

Then before the relative could ask any more questions, Chas said, "We have to go. We just stopped by to say hello, but we're on our way."

"Good," said Cousin Bart. "I'll go with you."

"Not this time." Chas smiled as he skillfully took Amy right on out of the busily chatting mob. "We'll be back for the dinner tonight," he said over his shoulder to those who tried to stop them, and the two escapees left.

"I've always read about running gauntlets," Amy walked on wobbly legs. "Was that one?"

"Very similar," Chas replied with amusement. "Instead of sharp sticks, they have sharp tongues. Some time you will see what they can do to *interlopers*."

Although he watched her with sparkling green eyes, he appeared not to notice her pale face, and he made no comment about her being discomforted by personal questions.

When they had safely reached the quadrangle, Amy shook her head and heaved a big, calming sigh. "Our family hasn't any relatives, and I've always been sorry—before—but now I'm not so sure."

"They're all just great," he promised. "Wait and see. In times of stress, they gather around and scold and argue. They demand special attentions, and they fix things. They're wonderful."

He seemed sure.

She was doubtful. She commented in censure. "The Cougars are so noisy! That's probably why the hotel put them on the sixth floor. Sound rises." Then she conceded, "They do appear to enjoy themselves." That was true, and Chas nodded. Laughter was the primary Cougar sound.

If they wouldn't question her, Amy would have liked to just stand around and listen among the guests for the wedding. Their conversations were startling, funny and filled with spicy or shocking remembrances. Nothing and no one was sacred.

The family really ought to tape their chatter. People and memories didn't last forever. Rather reluctantly she asked Chas, "Shouldn't you stay there? Be with them? We shouldn't just go off and leave everyone."

Chas shook his head as he smiled at Amy. "I see them several times a year. I know most of the stories. Tonight before dinner, we'll be with them at the cocktail gathering in the fountain area. Bart will probably fall in. He nips a bit."

"A bit?"

Chas laughed. "Quite a bit. He's a drunk. But he is the most loyal man you could ever find. When it comes right down to brass tacks, he's there . . . and sober."

"We've always just depended on ourselves."

"We do, too." Chas watched Amy. "But family support is a great thing."

"How about be*tween* emergencies?"

He grinned and ruffled her hair. "You are a treat. I agree with Bart. We should keep you."

She was a stickler. "Only through this weekend."

He took her hand. "We'll see."

She allowed him to hold her hand, but she began to think she might have to leave secretly. In order to do that, she should be reasonably packed, monitor how much she had in the suite, and be ready to take off on a minute's notice.

She'd have to leave a note. What would she say? "Nice knowing you"? That wouldn't ever convey the magic Chas had allowed her to know. What note could? What words?

His voice husky, he asked, "Whatever are you thinking that could be so serious on this glorious day?"

"About last night—with you."

"Oh, Amy." He stopped to put his arms around her and hold her tightly to him. "If you don't want to be put down right here on the drive, you'll have to be very careful. You drive me wild!"

She tilted up her face and teased, "I was thinking how much room you take up. I had to sleep on the very *very* edge! I've never realized what women put up with, sleeping with a man!"

"But you were warm," he told the sassy woman. "I woke up with you burrowing against me, and you said, 'Um, you're so warm!'" He tried to make his voice sound like hers and failed dismally.

He looked off into the distance and then around the area as men do. He told her, "If we want to go anywhere, we have to quit talking like this. You bother me. You have to... take it easy with me."

He had stressed the words, which were the title of the film on TV the night before, which they hadn't watched.

"Do you suppose that movie will be on again tonight?" she asked. "I'd like the chance to see it."

"I'll buy the tape. Eventually we might be able to get past the opening scene and watch it all."

"The movie set you off?" she asked with a frown.

"Something sure as hell did!" He changed the word, "Does. Let's go back to our place."

When she obediently turned back toward the hotel, she commented, "I thought we were going to drive down the coast."

Gesturing, he promised earnestly, "It looks just like this. Water, sky, sand, palm trees. No big deal. We could get a covered lounge and lie in the sun and rest up."

"I burn."

"I know," he sympathized. "You make me burn, too. You set me on fire."

"I believe you have a one-track mind. When I selected you . . . for this project, I had no idea you were a sex maniac."

"I never was before. What do you mean you selected me?"

"You know. To become . . . acquainted together." She blushed.

"You wanted to meet me?"

"Let's feed the gulls."

Intrigued, he questioned, "Are you shy with me?"

"I understand they'll eat about anything. There're some kids feeding them from their balcony. Probably their spinach."

"Hold still. I have to kiss you."

She gasped, "Out here! It's broad daylight!"

"Don't Aaabbotts kiss in the daytime?"

"You put too many *A*'s in it."

"That's how you say it."

"Be quiet and kiss me, or were you only threatening?"

So he showed her right there and then that he was serious. He kissed her for anyone around to see him do that. It didn't matter to him that everyone would guess.

All the Cougars knew the two were sharing a suite. No one believed the baloney that there were two sleeping areas.

They wandered around. He took her to a mall and bought her a hat with a rubber band under her chin to guard against the wind.

They rented poles and bought bait, before they walked out on a fishing pier. In no time at all, Chas caught two fish, which he gave away to a kid about eight years old.

Amy listened as Chas cautioned the boy to let his mother brag on the catch first, *then* to tell how he "caught" them.

The kid laughed with teeth big in his smile.

Amy contrived great censoring, saying, "You've trained the innocent child to lie!"

Chas smiled and nodded as he shrugged.

She said, "You're exactly the kind of man who'll teach a little innocent babe to do the raspberries with her tongue. And it'll take her mother a year and a half to break the baby of the habit."

He considered the premise with lifted eyebrows and nodded. "Yeah."

But it made Amy realize that Chas would be a good father.

He bought her sunscreen and put it on her face and arms. Then he squatted down and smoothed it on her legs with great care. He did that very slowly.

"I need to shave my legs." She was apologetic.

"I'll do it for you." His green eyes looked up at her from where he sat on his heels before her, holding her leg in his hands. "Amy..."

She smiled down at him.

He put one knee to the boardwalk, then leaned the side of his head against her stomach as he hugged her, with one big, hard hand at the small of her back and the other arm around her thighs.

She put her hands into his hair as a strange feeling smothered her chest, for she realized she could love this man.

He lifted his head, released her and went back to the application of sunscreen to her long legs.

"Me next!" a throaty female voice demanded.

"No, me," said another.

Chas apparently didn't hear, but Amy looked indignantly at the two shapeless women in their loose flowered shirts and soft rolled-up trousers.

The interlopers grinned widely at Amy.

But she didn't respond to them for—just beyond those two—there were younger women who had stopped and were watching Chas like buzzards.

Amy Abbott Allen, the man-izer, bristled and glared. She didn't show her teeth, but she thought of it.

Chas simply completed her legs' sun shield. He rose, surrounded by the cheerful group of watchers. He kissed Amy's forehead, took her hand and led her off as if he never saw anyone else.

He was an interesting man. A man. Oh, yes. After her thinking of baring her teeth, she was proud of the fact that she didn't look back over her shoulder and stick out her tongue.

She wasn't sure that not sticking out her tongue was any more adult than not baring her teeth.

As she contemplated her childish, primitive instincts, it eventually did register that she was allowing Chas to lead her along.

She was attached to him by his hand, which had captured hers, and she was walking about a pace behind him.

She considered that behavior. She was a Twenty-first Century Woman, independent and free. She was a man-izer. She was being led along very like a warrior's slave. She liked it.

That was sobering.

In the crowd of spring-break freed students and families with small children, Amy trailed along behind a Cougar who was breaking trail for her. She looked at him. She trusted him to keep her safe so that she was free to look around and to look at him.

His shoulders were wide and strong and his body was lean and hard. His torso had practically no bottom at all. He was walking at a reduced stride for her sake.

He turned his head and looked back around his shoulder and down at her. His eyelashes veiled the green fire in his eyes. He smiled just the littlest bit, and it was as if his tongue had licked her stomach in a big Cougar lap.

The sensation was such that she took an involuntary breath, as if he was about to submerge her in the pool, except there she was, on dry land.

Her eyes clung to him. She was suddenly aware her breasts felt heavy and ached oddly, for they needed to be lifted and held in his hands.

She was very conscious of the insides of her thighs. Unfamiliar muscles clenched, causing goose bumps to ride her spine, straightening it and raising the fine hairs along the way. All that from one of his glances!

No, there was his strong, hard, square hand holding hers firmly. There was his hard, broad shoulder brushing her cheek. There was the heat of him that rivaled the sun's and there was the fact that he was alive, there, and with her.

He looked around, not appearing to notice the women whose eyes lingered on him. He looked at her. She was with him. She was stalking along with a man named Chas Cougar.

Then into her consciousness a thwarted thought wormed its nasty way. Chas Cougar was a law-abiding man who hated cheats. Although she was with him, it was under false pretenses.

She'd lied. She'd cheated in opening a wedge into the Cougar clan, and she'd allowed herself to be labeled a cousin.

With all the feeble protests that she might not be kin, she hadn't denied it. There was that basic lie about her grandmother's name being Winsome. She'd allowed the false name to stay there...a lie.

"What's wrong?" His low voice was right by her temple.

She looked up into those green eyes in something like despair.

"Are you all right?" His voice was sharper, and he stopped to bend down, bringing his head closer so that he could look into her face. His other hand went to her shoulder and he frowned. "What's the matter?"

Her lips parted and she replied softly, "I guess I'm just a little tired."

"Good."

Good? He bought her a hamburger, led her back to their suite, muted the phone and took her to bed. This time in the bedroom. In one bed.

He moved away her shy, shielding hands and made delicious, possessive, silent, serious love to her, with his hard hands and his hard body. Then he curled her close in his arms and they slept.

Before she ever opened her eyes, she knew he was gone. Her lashes lifted and she confirmed that. He'd left her? She rose and looked in the closet. His clothes were still there. He would come back.

The relief that washed through her alarmed her almost as much as the panicked thought of his being gone. She could not allow herself to become emotionally entangled with a law-abiding man who despised cheats.

Now was the time to get her clothes organized for her vanishing act. She was convinced she would have to leave in that way. How could she stand in front of Chas—or lie next to him—and say goodbye? She put her hands in her hair and pulled.

This affair was dumb. It was an entrapment. She didn't want to leave, not yet, but would she ever want to leave him?

In her future affairs she was going to have to be more selective. Did that mean she would now choose second best? Surely not. She'd selected Chas because he was the best.

Her emotional involvement was probably because she'd been a virgin. There was a saying that women always felt sentimental about their first man. That was probably what was wrong with her. She was being sentimental about Chas.

She sorted out the clothes she would need for the night's cocktails and dinner, the next day and the wedding. And what she'd need when she left.

Amy dressed in a pullover cotton beach cover-up. She took her laundry, the extra clothes and shoes that had gradually found their way from her car to the shared closet. She picked up her card and sneaked out of the room to go to her car.

She even went around to the beachside elevator, in case Chas should be coming back up to their suite.

Having stored her burdens in her car, she wandered over the walkways and discovered a hidden stairway in which she could sit alone, unobserved, to figure out how she was going to handle leaving Chas.

She had barely settled on the step—there in the warmth of the sun—when she heard voices. She shifted, assuming they could come down the steps, but the voices stayed where they were, around the corner of the stairs. The voices were female and they continued their conversation.

The voices belonged to Connie and Sally.

Connie asked, "Why did you decide to marry Tad? Is he so different from all the others?"

"I'll tell *you* because of all we've been through together," Sally replied in an almost cynical way. "Last fall, I ran into a nice guy at a party. He was neat. I thought, 'Wow. All right!' and began to come on to him. And he said, 'So you do remember?'

"But I didn't. I found out I'd spent a *weekend* with him! An entire weekend, mostly in bed, and I couldn't even recall his *name!*

"He was offended, but I was appalled! There I'd slept with this guy for a whole weekend, and I didn't even remember his name.

"I figured it was time to quit. I'm fond of Tad. He loves me. I'll be careful of him, and I'll come to love him. You ought to consider settling down yourself, Connie. The fast track can last too long."

Connie's voice was faint. "I couldn't find a Tad. No one wants to actually marry me. They're all like Matt. I now have such a reputation that sleeping with me is like a goal along the way for men making their names as lovers."

"Burnout." Sally's voice was positive. "Take some time off until it's interesting again. I believe casual sex is like a drug. Used all the time it gets routine and hasn't the kick it should. Even druggies have to dry out before they then have another go at it."

Sally then advised Connie, "Take it easy for a while and let Matt sweat. It'll stimulate him, too.

"Ah, Connie, I'm glad you came down here. It seems appropriate for you to be here with me right now. You were there that first time, too."

Connie's voice was grim. "I'm not going to sleep with Matt."

"You don't want to?"

"I love him."

"So?"

"He doesn't love me." Connie's voice broke.

Sally's voice protested, "But he can't wait to get you into bed!"

"It wouldn't be the first time," Connie replied. "We've had a running affair for years. He's between women, and I'm handy."

Sally's voice asked soberly, "Is it really that way?"

"Yes."

"You're hurting!" Sally's voice was gentle.

"Badly."

"But you came to me, knowing he'd be here. Connie. You didn't hav— I can't even say it. You *had* to be here for me. You're the sister I never had."

"Yes." Connie's unstable voice agreed to that.

"Are you all right?"

The tone was bitter as Connie replied, "Fine."

"You know Tad wouldn't mind if you came along with us?"

Connie laughed in a hiccup. "Don't be ridiculous."

"That's better. I've another fitting for that infuriating gown! Want to come along?"

Connie's voice replied, "I think I'll walk a while."

"Then I'll see you later."

Amy thought they would never leave! She held perfectly still in the silence to be sure they had gone. Hearing nothing, she started to rise from her concealed nook.

Then she heard the muffled sobs. Amy hesitated. How could she leave Connie there so alone and unhappy?

Amy remembered all the times she'd cried alone. She had especially poignant understanding when Chas said how the Cougars rallied around a distressed member.

She was a Cougar! However temporarily. She would just go and be with Connie like a sober cousin Bart.

As Amy went silently up the stairs, she hesitated with the realization that she was intruding. Connie didn't hear her. She was sitting, curled in a ball on the top step. Her face buried in her hands. Her blond hair was a lovely tumble.

Amy stood helplessly, then sat down next to Connie and said, "Need a friend's—a cousin's Kleenex?"

Connie jerked her head up, her tear-red eyes wide and startled, then she leaned against Amy and simply bawled.

Amy gave Connie the Kleenex as she put her arms around her. A good cry can clear thinking. But she waited, and Connie didn't stop. She was shuddering in spasms.

Amy asked softly, "What could be this bad? Whatever it is, you can survive it. Come now. You can't allow yourself to be this upset. How can I help you? Are you ill?"

Connie nodded vigorously and made a harsh sound as she shivered.

Lumps or bleeding? Amy asked in dread, "Have you seen a doctor?"

"Tomorrow."

"Don't anticipate trouble. Do you want me to go with you?"

Connie moved away from Amy and looked at her with a ravaged face. "Oh, Amy, thank you! At nine-thirty. I couldn't go to my own doctor. I'd die."

"Where shall I meet you?"

A deep, masculine voice, so recently become familiar, asked as he squatted down on the wooden walkway behind the two women, "What's going on?"

It was Chas. It was as if the marines had landed. "Connie? Trouble? Tell me."

"I can't." With some effort Connie brought herself under stern control. She straightened and calmed herself.

Chas gave Connie a clean handkerchief. He took Amy's elbow as he rose, encouraging her to stand up. He said to Amy, "We'll see you at our suite, okay? It won't be long." He kissed Amy's cheek and patted her bottom discreetly. She had been dismissed.

Amy looked down at Connie, who had also risen and would have moved down the steps, but Chas had her arm in his other hand, and she wasn't going anywhere. "Is this okay?" she asked Connie.

"Yes." Connie even almost smiled. "Chas is relentlessly helpful."

"Do you want him to interfere?" Amy felt all powerful.

Connie shrugged. "He will, anyway. We might as well let him."

Amy gave Chas a cool glance, and he winked at her.

How like a man not to realize he'd been snubbed. She turned away as she flipped her body around and strode off down the walkway.

She didn't immediately go back to their suite, but walked independently around for a while before she admitted that whatever was Connie's problem, Chas would handle it. He was a man who could solve things, ease them, cope.

Connie was lucky she had Chas to turn to. It was just that he appeared to be a dominant male Cougar, and everything was under his control and his way. It rankled . . . her.

But Connie really needed him. Under those circumstances, Amy could allow Chas to take over and solve whatever it was.

Even if she wasn't being deliberately disobedient to Chas—who had told her to go and wait for him—she couldn't immediately go back to the suite. There was an unsettling mishmash for her to digest.

Amy headed out to the beach and walked. She waved in reply to greetings from her ersatz cousins, and she called Chas's evasive, "Later," to invitations to join groups either sitting in the sun or playing beach ball. She needed to be alone.

She walked on beyond the last of their hotel's residents, so she could mull over what she'd inadvertently heard between Sally and Connie. Sexual burnout? Job burnout was common, drug burnout, but sexual burnout?

It probably wasn't the sex. It was the machinations of finding someone acceptable, going through the preliminaries and then finding ways to separate.

Amy could understand that. It was horrendous! She had been a mess of nerves and hesitations before she finally got Chas into bed. Just the sweat of doing all that could get old fast. Sleeping with him, making love to him had been marvelous...delicious.

But now she was facing the necessity of saying goodbye to him and leaving. And *he* was saying, "We'll see." It could be difficult to shake him off.

She'd ask Sally how to say goodbye. Sally would know. She'd had so many affairs, she'd not even remembered one man. A whole weekend! And Sally had forgotten.

Amy knew she'd always remember Chas. If she was more experienced, she might consider a serious relationship with him. Even marriage.

But why shouldn't she sow some wild oats? That was an interesting saying. Sowing wild oats meant illegitimate children. And for men, it was wild oats, but for women it was one-parent children.

She wouldn't do that to a child. Obviously she was going to have to learn more about birth control, being discreet and how to tactfully say goodbye without hurting feelings or letting the man feel he'd been discarded instead of simply, casually tasted.

How did men handle this tactfully? She had read tales of those men who were harsh and cruel, but surely all men weren't hurtful. She needed more information.

Anything men could do, she could do, but she would do it better. She wasn't the ordinary woman. She was no different than any man.

Six

As Amy walked back to the Trade Winds, she turned her thoughts to Connie. She was how old? Thirty? She and Sally were about the same age. How many men had they slept with?

At night when they couldn't sleep, did they count their conquests, like sheep over a fence?

Maybe not, if Sally hadn't even remembered at least one man. Had she forgotten others?

That seemed strange. It had even shocked Sally. Amy swore, right then, that she would be selective. She would pick and choose her bedmates wisely.

She wouldn't just hop into bed, she would be discriminating to the extent that each experience would be separate in her mind, and she *would* remember.

What about Connie? She was very seriously scared. What was wrong? What if she had something horrendous? Something unsolvable.

Chas could handle the brunt of that for Connie and help her to bear it. He could handle anything. With the acceptance that Chas was in control, Amy finally went back to the suite, as directed, to wait for Chas.

She opened the suite door, and he was there. He smiled at her as if he understood perfectly why she'd absented herself for a token period in a show of defiance.

She narrowed her eyes at him because she had amused him. "Connie?" she inquired, raising her eyebrows politely, but she really wanted to know.

"Better," he replied. "You were very sweet to her. I was searching for you when Sally said Connie might need me. She didn't. You were there." He came to Amy and, without touching her, he leaned and very gently kissed her mouth.

Chas hadn't said he'd been looking for her, he used the word "searching," which was a different, more doggedly intense manner of finding. Search was more thorough. Perhaps even a little relentless?

It was a strange choice of words. Search. Search and find.

The use of the word gave her an odd feeling in her feminine core. It became a little panicky, like a woman in a forest with a man following her scent. Chas looked the part of a hunting man.

When he ended the kiss and lifted his head, his green eyes smiled into her serious blue ones. He said, "I found the gift to remind you of me. I was looking for a slave collar, but there aren't any of those readily available. So I found this."

He opened a small velvet box and took out a platinum chain with a single, luminous pearl.

He told her, "The pearl is from the sea. And it was here by the sea that we came together."

She was speechless. Like "search" he said "we came together" instead of met . . . as if there would be no parting.

She wondered if he chose the words deliberately, or if she was just sensitive to the fact that he didn't conduct himself like an object but appeared as if he thought he was in command.

He opened the clasp, put the chain around her throat and closed the clasp again. There was the tiniest sound, but why did it sound like a period on a document?

"There's a safety," Chas told her. "You'll have to turn it so you can unclasp it, or you can take it off over your head. I got the chain a little long." He centered the clasp of the chain at the center of her nape, then he judiciously observed as the pearl settled between her breasts. "I guessed right." He was pleased. Any man who looked at her chest would see his pearl.

She looked down at the pearl as she told him, "I can't keep it. It's too expensive."

"I got it at a thrift store," he stated with the most open, candid look. "It was quite reasonable."

She considered him uncertainly.

"It's one you may keep," he assured her.

But she knew pearls. She lifted it, knowing that her skin's oil had already affected the color of it.

It was gorgeous. The chain was a lovely, intricately linked work of art. And *he'd* said he hated liars.

What about men who discounted costly gifts? Like a pearl drop on an unusually contrived, platinum chain?

"It's beautiful," she told him. Then she kissed him.

Chas hugged her tightly. He was so pleased with himself. Amy decided she would wear it for the next two, too-brief days. No harm in that.

But she would leave it behind when she vanished. To keep such a gift would change their interlude into paid sex, and she could be termed a whore.

Still holding her to him, his face moving around her head in a slow, extraordinarily charming manner, he asked, "What are you wearing tonight?"

"The blue dress."

He lifted his head to frown at her. "When I came back, I looked at that dress. I believe you could pull it through a ring. Is it decent enough for tonight? I don't want to have to fight off all the men over fourteen years old who are there and see you in that dress." He gave her a mock-irritated scowl.

She smiled because he expected her to, but she thought, so he had looked to see if her clothes were still there? Just as she had looked for his.

How insecure they both were. What would he have done if her clothes had been gone? And she vividly recalled his word "search."

His voice a husky whisper, he coaxed, "Let me bathe you."

In some shock, she protested, "We'd never get to the cocktail party."

He grinned and lied, "I have iron control."

"You told me you weren't an iron man. That's why you didn't leave me alone when you found out you were my first. It was only after that you said I shouldn't be fooling around."

"With—any—one—else." He spaced the words as he added to her sentence.

"I have heard men say that to women. They tumble women as they choose, but they tell the women to behave. Why is that?" It suddenly occurred to her that she might learn from Chas.

Very kindly, he instructed, "Men never 'tumble' women. We are all victims of voracious female appetites."

"That's why you moved in here?" She lifted her eyebrows in subtle disbelief.

He nodded emphatically and instructed, "I realized you were a novice, and I simplified the whole operation for you."

"How kind."

He nodded in serious acceptance of her droll appreciation, moving his hand out in an open gesture. He casually elaborated, "I thought it was important for you to succeed on your first try."

She tilted her head back so that she could look at him directly. "How did you know I was a novice? The only thing that panicked you was how old I was. Is there a way for men to know when women are virgins?"

He explained logically, "Outside the obvious one, you didn't lean your breast against me and bare your teeth up at me."

She scoffed as she replied, "You make women sound shockingly predatory! Teeth?"

"It's a jungle out there." Then he sighed in long suffering.

"You could have said 'smiled' up at you."

"Teeth. That's all a man sees. Teeth turned his way. It's frightening. I have astonishing nightmares." He made his voice earnest. "I wake up in a sweat after some of those dreams." He gave her a sad, quite sly look.

"Of teeth?" she guessed drolly.

"Partly." He nodded slowly, but those crinkles around his eyes deepened.

Suddenly, she guessed, "You're a fraud." And she knew he was fooling her.

"Now Amy Aaaabbott, how can you say that?"

Her eyes flew open, and she had trouble not jerking in surprise. Why had he said those extra A's right then? Was he implying *she* was a fraud?

He had to know, or he would never have said her false name at that particular time! He was playing a game with her?

How could he possibly know she wasn't exactly who and what she said she was? He couldn't. Not *possibly!* It was her own guilty conscience.

She took over their conversation, changing the subject to one that would surely distract his thoughts of fraud. "I shall bathe you." That ought to catch his attention. "This is my suite, my weekend. I am in control. Speaking of control, Chas, why did Connie say you always took control, and we would just have to let you?"

"We're cousins. Connie's a year older than I, and she's never forgiven me for growing taller. She is a very domineering woman." Quietly serious, he told Amy, "She's also something of a tart. I'd never admit that to an outsider, but the entire family knows of her indiscretions.

"I . . . we have other cousins you'd find better company. Some are here. Sharan, Kim, Ann. There are a lot of very nice women in our family."

"You came to Connie to help her," she reminded him.

He nodded. "Family obligation." Then he looked levelly at Amy.

"You don't like her?"

"I . . . I'm her cousin. We grew up knowing each other. We have many memories in common. She's family. I help where and how I can."

Amy asked, "Are you going with her tomorrow?"

"Yes."

"What's wrong with her?"

Chas replied gently, "We'll know tomorrow."

"Can I help?"

"You already did. You were very sweet." He put his hand along her jaw and tilted her face to his. "I saw you in that nook and watched as you decided to help. You could have left because she didn't know you were there.

"I would bet my soul that your hesitation was because you weren't sure about intruding. But Connie was really hurting, and you went to her. I like you, Amy."

She put her hands up to slide her fingers into his thick black hair. "Have you ever slept with her?"

He shook his head. "She's a cousin."

Amy shrugged. "So is Matt."

"That's different."

"How?"

"It just is." Then to dismiss the whole subject, Chas said, "So you want to bathe me? How do I dare trust my tender, naked body to a declared user of strange men? Do you really want to get me clean or are you just using that as an excuse to get your hands on me? Are you a lecher?"

"I'll be gentle."

He laughed, so amused with her. He hugged her tightly to him. "I hope I can last a decent amount of time. Is this plain or with soap bubbles?"

She was generous about it. "Which would you prefer?"

"Showers with strong walls."

She put her head back to laugh as he picked her up and carried her around the suite just for the pleasure of holding her and carrying her. He was so strong.

He teased her, tilting her as if to dump her on her head, making her clutch and squeal. He carried her, pretending to falter, turning her in circles, taking her to the bed . . . and making love to her.

They showered together. He was careful with her body. Serious. Diligent. She stretched and turned as she allowed it, and he warned her, "Be careful."

He mostly bathed himself in quick scrubbings, not nearly so carefully done, and she leaned back to watch him with a tender smile. He took her from the tub, dried her with concentration, then dried her hair, but she had to help with the brushing. He tended to curry hair.

He was ridiculously, enormously relieved she wore underwear beneath the flimsy blue dress! She was a little indignant, "You expected me to go out in public with just this dress? And *nothing* else?"

He completely ignored all her indignation to ask, "Sometime will you wear it that way just for me?"

"Chas, for Pete's sake! I would feel like a . . . tart!" She had sought for his word of censure.

"With me, it's all right for you to be one. Not with anyone else."

She made an impatient sound and pulled the dress on over her head. She shook her dried hair in a swirl, and Peter's perfect cut fell automatically into place.

Chas watched her. "I love your hair. It's sable. I shall buy you a coat that exact color."

"No."

"Yes." He observed her judiciously. "Will you let it grow long for me? I would like to see it down your back."

"I leave on Sunday."

"We'll see."

She turned and gave him an impatient look, but he only smiled at her. Then he pulled his shirt on over his wide shoulders and came to her with his cuff links.

She took his cuff and began to work the links into their holes, and his fingers moved to touch her chest. Primly, she tightened her mouth as she said, "Behave."

"Why do women always say that to their men?" He was cocky. He was so confident, so teasingly sure.

"Because they're always out of hand."

He laughed, holding up his hands. "I'm not out of hands. See? I still have some left."

How would she be able to leave him in a mature way with a plain goodbye? Why couldn't he be adult about this? Casual.

With his attitude, he'd probably get mad when she left. He'd be furious!

He was so sure she wasn't going to leave him. He acted as if he intended to keep her around as long as he wanted her.

This talk about a fur, and her growing her hair long. That took time, and a fur wouldn't be appropriate until next winter. It was only March. He was thinking long-term.

She finished the cuff links and said, "There."

"You do that well."

"How many women have done that for you?"

"My mother, my cherished sister. A cousin. No unrelated women."

His green eyes appeared honest. He was a vibrant, potent thirty-year-old. Was it possible he could be that age and never have lived with any woman? "Have you ever lived with a woman?"

"Just here, with you."

"Ah." That explained it. He hadn't yet and he thought she might be a good candidate for the trial? No way.

"Ah. What's that mean?"

"I just wondered."

He narrowed his eyes a trifle. "What sort of wondering did the fact that I haven't lived with a woman satisfy?"

"Just that."

He frowned at the slippery-minded woman. "You make me uneasy. I'm not familiar with female thinking. What are you thinking?"

She smiled at him and tilted her head as she touched his cheek. "I like green eyes."

"Evasive. What are you thinking?"

"We'll see." Those, too, were words he had used.

"You're becoming enigmatic, and I'm becoming very nervous about you, Amy. What's going on in that busy little brain of yours? Don't you do anything without telling me. Do you hear me?"

"I need to put on my makeup. Will that be all right?"

"Don't be sassy. Sassy girls get what's coming." He crowded her with his body.

She tilted up her nose in the sassiest way she could, being new at that, too. She replied, "You don't scare me. Not for another hour, anyway!"

"I travel light and this is the only other tux shirt I have with me. But don't let that make you reckless, woman." His eyes were squinted, his jaw was forward and his eyes danced with his laughing threats.

She tilted her own jaw up sideways and looked at him from under long lashes. "Please, please, Mr. Wolf, don't eat me up." Her voice lacked any real conviction.

He deepened his voice awesomely and replied, "All right, Little Red Riding Hood, but your old grandmother was only skin and bones, and I'm still hungry."

"Pooh," she said as she picked up her makeup kit and deliberately swished her hips as she passed him. She looked back, and he was watching her with a smug smile.

He looked up to her watching eyes, and he took a long step and swatted her bottom. "That's what happens to sassy women."

"Oh!" she said elaborately surprised. "I was afraid of something else entirely!"

His green eyes glinted. "That, too."

She was bending over the lavatory with her face next to the mirror as she put on her mascara when, dressed, he came to lean in the doorway to watch her. She ignored him and continued her makeup.

Finished, she turned toward him, and he was simply gorgeous in his formal clothing. He said, "You were already perfect."

"Will you do this?" She handed him the chain with its lovely pearl.

"You're going to wear it?" He was inordinately pleased. "My thrift-shop pearl with that lovely gown?"

"I think the dress will hide it."

"Not that dress." He clasped the lock and deliberately leaned around her shoulder to watch the pearl slowly slide down into place.

She *tsked* her tongue once as if in irritation and complained, "The neck's too low. The pearl shows. Darn."

He dipped his fingers into the neckline, nudging the rounds that met there. "If the chain was a little bit longer, these would keep the pearl polished and glowing."

She held the pearl, looking at it. Then she looked up at him and told him, "It's a beautiful pearl."

"So are you."

She tilted her head back and considered him. "You're an awesome man. I wish I'd already had my fill of other men."

He almost smiled as he told her confidently, "You have. You just haven't realized it, yet."

"How could I have my fill when you're my first?"

He spread his hand openly. "You don't need any other men. I'm all you need."

"Nonsense."

"Can I kiss you?"

"Carefully."

* * *

The cocktail party was a noisy, laughing, sluggishly moving maelstrom. "So this is the...new 'cousin.'" The betraying quotes were obvious even in speech.

Quite boldly Amy said to Chas, "They don't believe I'm a cousin." She told him that just to see what he would reply.

Since he was honest, would he tell the truth and agree with his relatives? She watched his lips as they said, "In good time, they'll get used to the idea."

A tactful nothing reply.

Kenneth came along through the crowd to say, "Hello, Cousin Amy, I'm sure you missed me terribly, especially with this hunk blundering around and embarrassing you with his domineering edicts? You need a calmer man who will allow you some breathin—"

It was Chas who interrupted, "That's enough, Ken, don't push me. Did you see what's-his-name?"

Kenneth said in an aside to Amy, "An excellent example of exactly what I was saying." He then raised his eyebrows and looked down his nose at Chas. "Yes. I saw Martin Durwood. He is exactly what Amy warned. I was discreet. I left things vague until we can discuss how to handle this." He looked at Amy. "I counted my fingers twice to be sure. I owe you one for the warning. He's a very smooth and dangerous man."

Amy nodded in agreement. "Avoid him."

"We may have to deal with him, but forewarned is forearmed, and we are. What would you like for the warning? A piece of the pie?"

Both men watched her with seeming casualness. They couldn't miss the fact that she was startled by the words. "Of course not! The warning was given as a friend."

Chas rubbed his nose to hide his pleasure, and Ken smiled at her. "We take your favor seriously. Our thanks."

Kenneth stayed around until Chas asked him, "Why don't you get lost?"

"Rejected?" Kenneth was astounded. "No, you consider me a threat? How nice of you. Keep me in mind, Amy. He gets dull fast."

Chas said nicely, "I may throw you off the balcony."

Kenneth told Amy, "See? Pay attention, dear cousin. A violent, possessive man. I'll withdraw discreetly, but I'll be around if you should need any aid against such a Neanderthal." He lifted his fist to his face so that his thumb touched his nose as he laughed at Chas, and went off into the crowded room.

Chas felt the need to tell Amy, "He doesn't mean any of it, other than that about Durwood. He does mean that. But the rest of it is pure Kenneth hype. Don't pay any attention to him."

She responded, "Yes, sir." But her tone wasn't really that subservient.

"See? Your whole attitude is improving."

Sally came past in the crowd and told Amy not to forget the hen party after dinner. She whispered it to Amy. "This is a limited gathering. Don't mention it. Come to Connie's room. Okay?"

"I'll be there."

Sally gave Amy a quick hug, then she kissed Chas. He turned his head so that her mouth missed his.

Sally pretended she meant only to salute his cheek, and she wiggled away in the crowd.

"What was that about?" Chas wanted to know.

"I guess it's supposed to be a secret. I've already told you, so don't you mention it to anyone. The hen party."

Chas countered her sternly, "Don't eat or drink anything. Say you're full."

He was warning her about drugs? "They wouldn't do anything that stupid."

"Do as I say." He was quite stern.

Annoyed, she breathed another, snide, "Yes, *sir!*"

He grinned at her. "I like that. I like an obedient woman."

She snorted indignantly and turned her back on him. It only amused him.

He was never far from her. He never let her get entangled with a group for too long. That's murderous at a cocktail party. One never sits down or stays with any one group.

And knowing his family, he didn't want the doubters to peck at her.

It was at this time that Amy noticed Chas never kissed women on the mouth. He managed to avoid it. She'd seen Sally try to kiss him, and thought it was just that Sally was a bride-to-be, and he was acknowledging that with a hands-off sort of attitude. But now she realized he simply did not kiss women on their mouth. Other women. He kissed her mouth.

Amy realized her father was the same way. He never greeted women he knew with hugs and kisses. He was nice about greetings and liked women, but he simply did not hug or kiss them. Chas was that way, too?

With the press of the crowd, it was Chas's shoulder that protected her from being jostled, and it was he who saw to it that she had water instead of wine. That made her somewhat indignant.

He explained quite nicely, "You're not going to have champagne with the toasts. I can't stand drinking women."

She leaned back so she would observe him in censorship. "What about you?"

He lifted his glass. "Water." But then he reminded her, "I'm driving." He grinned at her then.

So he wasn't a lush? Neither was her father. How many times had her dad said that booze kills brain cells and he needed all his. But Chas had given her wine with the pizza the night she first seduced him.

Eventually the crowd moved to the dining room and were seated. There were a lot of them. How marvelous so many of the family could come there to this elegant place. How strange the couple wasn't to be married in their home church.

But Amy gradually learned, in the babble of chatter, that not too many of them lived, now, where they'd grown up.

They were part of the job mobility that had scattered much of the population after World War II, and such mobility had continued as if that was the way to live. Their old home town was plural.

Amy noted Connie. As maid of honor, she had to be there. She was so quiet in that animated group. She looked finely honed. It must be hell for her, waiting for what the doctor would tell her the next day. What could it be to rattle such a woman?

Thinking of Connie made Amy consider how many people she met—as she moved around in her work, and now with this impulsive joining with strangers—

and how strange it was to become involved in concern for other people.

Traveling was broadening.

It made Amy realize what an enviable facade we put on people of affluence. We believe their lives are magic. Perfect. And we look on those who have no means at all with only a sense of responsibility, our compassion tempered with irritation because they can't straighten themselves out.

But as Kipling wrote about the Colonel's Lady and Rosey O'Grady, we are all sisters under the skin. All of us struggle and have problems. And Connie was suffering.

The toasts were hilarious. Some were old family treasures that Chas had to try to explain, but were senseless to outsiders. Matt was sitting next to Connie, and he toasted, "The winner." Was he just a little cynical?

But Tad's reply toast was, "To the losers." He was no fool.

Amy wondered if Sally really appreciated Tad. Given only what Amy knew, what were the chances for the marriage between Sally and Tad to survive?

What about Connie? And Matt? Matt appeared solicitous and attentive to Connie. Paying dues to get her into bed?

And Amy wondered, was that what Chas was doing to her? Insuring a bed partner? He, too, was attentive and solicitous. Charmingly so. But not treating her with any kind of equality.

He was the courteous male to an attractive female.

Did he ever acknowledge that females were capable of anything any male could do? Did he work well with women? What difference did that make to her?

In about thirty-six hours, she would be gone.

Seven

"Skip the hen party." That was the first thing Chas said to Amy after they left the bachelor's dinner and were walking toward their suite.

"Aren't you going with Tad and the rest?"

"Remember? I told you I was driving tonight. I have to see to it these fools don't wrap a car around something. I have to go."

"Have to?" Amy chose to repeat those two words. "That's not very enthusiastic."

Chas explained, "I've outgrown bachelor bashes. I've been to too many. They're all just alike. Drinking, dirty jokes and trashy films. A stripper. An adolescent coming-of-age that clings like barnacles to a fine tradition."

Then he stopped Amy to say, "This hen party is a female copy. It will offend you. Don't go."

Declining his advice, Amy scoffed. "I've been to several of these with sorority sisters, and they were fun!"

"You were all younger."

She demurred, "I'm not that old."

"I know. But I also know these particular cousins. This segment. You don't belong with them. Don't go. The group that'll be there tonight is—uh—well, tried. You don't want this experience with this bunch."

"I can't *not*," she explained. "Sally asked me. There aren't going to be very many there. She included me over her cousins!" Then Amy hastened to mend her careless words. "Uh...other cousins she...knows better. I'm new. I'm flattered. I think it would be rude to simply not show up."

Chas narrowed his eyes and his voice was soft but firm. "They will ask you about...sleeping with me...and..."

"Don't be silly! Who would do that?"

He assured Amy, "It will come up gradually. They'll confess to experiences, they start matching bed hops, and they'll invite you to join in."

"Women aren't like men! They won't do anything of the sort! You're accusing them of something a long way beyond kiss-and-tell."

"Don't tell," he urged. "It's none of their business."

"I know that! What do you take me for? I'm surprised you feel you must advise me on something so basic."

He didn't quit. He warned, "Don't let them trick you into any confessions or confidences. Nothing you do is any of their business."

"I know that!" she shouted and waved her arms around. "I find it very offensive that you don't trust me! You're making me angry."

Almost gently, Chas told her, "This is something to be angry about. I only mean to warn you. You're a very nice woman, Amy. You don't realize how women can be."

"I'm not such an innocent. I've traveled quite widely, and I've met a good many people. I've learned to judge people and I know how to conduct myself."

"You're a lady. You haven't been thrown into a pool of barracudas. You need to be warned so you can protect yourself"

She flung out her hands and snapped, "I'm warned! Now leave off!"

He stood with his hands low on his lean hips and watched her. He reached one big hand out and cupped the side of her head, but she resisted being drawn to him. He shook her head a little, and he said, "Behave."

She clenched her fists and made a tight-lipped, furiously frustrated sound, then she flipped around to go to the elevator, but he followed her. They went up to the sixth floor. He escorted her to Connie's door and knocked for her, watching her, his face still. Amy refused to lift her glance to his.

Was she angry enough? He sure as hell hoped so. He was very reluctant for her to attend this gathering of these particular cousins. He'd handled her all wrong.

He should have told Sally that Amy wouldn't be there. He should have made it plain. Or he should have refused to drive tonight and cajoled Amy into going with him ... swimming in the late night.

Beach walking in the moonlight? He should have paid more attention. He had to go and drive that bunch. He'd promised. Damn.

It was Connie who opened the door. Chas didn't smile. He said to Connie's greeting, "I'll see you about eight tomorrow morning? You'll want to have breakfast first?"

Connie shook her head. The circles under her eyes were dark, and she looked terrible.

So Chas told Connie, "Then I'll see you about nine. Is that okay? That'll give us plenty of time."

She nodded and said quietly, "Thanks, Chas."

Having reminded Connie that he was doing her a favor, Chas demanded one of his own. He leaned his head forward a little, for emphasis, as he told her in tones that couldn't be mistaken, "You take care of Amy."

Connie looked briefly startled, but she said, "Yes."

Chas didn't leave it there. He added, "See to it!"

Connie smiled slightly then, and agreed, "Right." But she added a serious, "I shall."

Amy could have died. He treated her like a twelve-year-old who needed a keeper.

Still talking to Connie, Chas said, "We'll come by later."

"Don't be too long."

"I'll try," Chas promised. "These things can last forever."

Sally came down the walkway. "Hey!" She smiled and wrapped an arm around Chas's neck. "Want to stay with us? It'd be lots more fun!"

"You all behave yourselves." Chas removed Sally from him.

Amy thought he was woodenly obnoxious. However, she also noted that Sally had leaned her breast against Chas and showed her teeth exactly the way he said women did to him.

It was then Amy realized Sally wanted Chas! And given the chance, she would sleep with Chas that very night! She was going to marry Tad tomorrow, but Sally wanted Chas. The realization did more to warn Amy than any of Chas's irritating lectures.

Chas ignored the other two women as he said to Amy, "We shouldn't be overly long. They're agreeable drunks and can be led."

Amy shrugged, still a little hostile.

Chas smiled and put a hand around her nape and growled softly in her ear so that only she heard. He told her, "I could throttle you."

That incensed Amy!

She puffed as Sally laughed. "What'd he say?"

Chas replied, "I told her to behave."

Sally hooted, "There go the tapes!"

"Wear a blindfold." He leaned and kissed Amy before she could back away. He grinned at her. "I'll try to get them back in a reasonable time." He lifted a hand to the other two in farewell, and he left.

Amy followed her two "cousins" into Connie's room, feeling like Danielle Entering The Lioness's Den. How silly. For something to say, Amy asked, "Why did he keep saying they wouldn't be long?"

"They're coming here after they've gone a few places. It'll be a couple of hours."

The other two of the select guests did come. Charlotte and Kate. They were a little older than thirty. Their eyes were wiser.

Their language slid into words Amy didn't use even to exclaim inside her mind. But she was young yet. Would the time come when she would use such words so casually?

Connie's room had a wet bar, and Sally mixed strong drinks. Paying attention to Chas's other warning, Amy said, "Later. I'm still woozy from all the toasts."

"Good time to top it off!" Sally mixed her a drink anyway.

Since Amy was twenty-four, she wasn't pushed into even sipping the drink, she could set it down and ignore it.

Sally and her cousins chatted and laughed, catching up on news.

Connie wasn't as outgoing.

Charlotte asked her, "What's the matter?"

Connie was evasive. "Just tired."

Charlotte then asked, salaciously laughing, "Matt been at you?"

That got a round of laughs.

Connie shaped her lips exactly and just said the word, "No."

Then even Charlotte and Kate asked seriously, "Are you okay, Connie? Do you need any help?"

"Thanks, no."

There were variations of, "We're here." The newcomers were serious as they looked at Connie soberly.

Connie replied softly, "I know. Thanks."

But then the rowdiness began. Sally had a videocassette recorder and played a tape. It was a specific film, short and explicit.

Amy blushed scarlet and her eyes popped.

The three others laughed and gave stage directions and appeared rather familiar with the film, for their directions anticipated what would happen.

Connie and Amy just watched. Connie was silent and distracted. Amy was shocked. Why would women allow themselves to be filmed that way? Or men.

After the film, the watchers began the round of men the cousins had known—and loved. Sally set it off. "He reminds me of Sam. I couldn't *believe* him!"

Chas had been right. He had known exactly how they'd behave.

Sally urged replenished drinks, and they saw another film. Amy looked away. She wished she'd listened to Chas. What a way to spend time.

With the end of each short film, the conversational memories of the women became more explicit. They matched and competed sexual experiences the way people in a doctor's office compare and top operations, complications, fevers and sicknesses. It was very similar.

Finally Sally said, "The only regret I have, in my spotted career of manhunting, is that I've never managed to get Chas to chase me."

Sally looked at Amy with an encouraging smile. "But *you* managed! How did you do it?" And her voice held great admiration as she went on, "I tried every trick I've learned on him and he tells me, 'Behave yourself!' I told him today that tonight was his last chance. After tonight, I'm going to be true to Tad. You know what Chas said? He said, 'See that you do.'"

They all laughed. Even Connie smiled. Then Kate and Charlotte related their strategies in trying to trap Chas. All of which, as they told it, were near misses.

But the stories had a carefully honed sound. They were very clever.

And there was much laughter. Amy looked at them as if they were aliens. How could Chas have predicted this would happen so exactly? How had he managed to escape their clutches?

So Sally asked, "Amy, how did you get Chas into bed?"

Blunt.

When Amy could catch her breath, she asked, "Why do you ask such a question?"

"Well, we all tried and failed, but you got him that first night! How did you do it?"

Their eyes were all turned to her as they waited. They wanted to hear. She hesitated, then said, "Ask him." He'd tell them it wasn't any of their business. "Tell him I said to ask him."

Sally persisted, "Is he good? I've never even seen him naked. How *is* he?"

Amy understood by then that she could never consult with any of them on how to say goodbye to Chas. She inquired quite primly, "Where are you and Tad going to live?"

Connie said, "Brava!"

"Come on, cousin, tell us." It was Charlotte who gave Sally support by pressing for Amy's reply. "How did Chas go about it? Was he clever or did he just tell you to strip and hop into bed?"

"Are you going to keep your job?" Amy inquired of Sally.

Remembering her promise to Chas, Connie took a hand, as she told the others, "Leave her alone."

"She's the only one I've ever known who's slept with Chas." Kate argued. "What's she got?"

Connie continued to interfere. "Shall we order up snacks? My treat."

"Who can eat?"

Amy inquired of Sally, "Are you nervous?"

"If you really want to know, I'll tell you, but then you'll have to tell me about Chas. I'll trade. I'll tell you how Tad is, if you'll tell me what it's like with Chas."

Amy replied stiffly, "It's private. I'm not interested in hearing about Tad. That's private."

Charlotte mocked Amy, "Goody Two-Shoes."

Amy laughed. "Yes."

Kate dismissed Amy, "You're no Cougar."

Amy stared.

But then Connie told the others, "There are more of her kind than there are of us. You can see that quite clearly when you consider all the cousins of our age who aren't here with us tonight. Actually, I begin to envy her."

Sally was suddenly stilled.

But Kate retorted, "You're mad. I wouldn't give up one. Not one. They were all marvelous!"

"Of course!" Charlotte agreed, but her support was somewhat dry as she added, "Even the rotten ones."

Sally protested, "Don't let's talk about the dreadful ones. I get depressed enough."

"How about the fumblers?" Connie put in.

Amy listened to them and wondered how much genetics had to do with their behavior. They said Trilby had only been eccentric. Of course, there had been the kinswoman, Letty, whose scandalous behavior had barred her from her place in the family burial plot. When that story was told, someone had said all Cougars had a strong attraction for the opposite sex.

It was Kate who set her glass down as she said, "Men have it tough."

"Yeah." Sally sighed and flopped back in her chair in a sprawl. "With women it's inexperience, but men can't ever be unskilled."

"Oh, I don't know." Kate stretched her nice body rather elaborately. "I had a young one two weeks ago, and I had a good time instructing him."

"How young?" Sally inquired with interest.

"Quite young, but old enough."

It was Connie who again commented, "You sound like old witches counting scalps."

Sally said, "Speaking of the talent for getting scalps. Tonight I'm passing on my green dress. You four are the most skilled of all the cousins.

"Amy, I included you because you're the only one of us who has ever snagged Chas. That puts you right up here with us. I don't know how many others you've had, but having Chas is clout. And so it's to you that I'm giving the green dress."

Sally got up and brought the dress from her closet. It was a beauty. Amy remembered hearing that Sally had worn it with some guy named Frank. If Sally's wedding dress hadn't arrived, she couldn't substitute the green one because she couldn't think of Frank when she was being married to Tad.

This was a successful, man-snaring gown. Proven. It would come in very handy in Amy's man-izing career. Wait until Chas saw her in that! She took the dress as she said, "Why, Sally, thank you."

Sally kissed her cheek. "Maybe when you and Chas break up, you'll tell me. I can understand your being loyal, right now, when it's new between you, but I will go wild until I know what I missed."

Amy looked at her incredulously. "You'll have Tad."

"He's sweet, but he isn't Chas. Put on the dress and let's see how you'll look." They laughed because Amy went into the bathroom to change.

When she emerged, they whistled and applauded.

Sally said, "I may have created a monster. No man will say no to you in that dress."

Amy was astonished by Sally's comment. How interesting they recognized her as one of them. How had they known? It was quite apparent they'd known all along. Was it Chas moving in that had alerted them? Or was there now some look about her that they recognized?

Amy said with respect, "The dress is gorgeous." And it was. It was sea green. Blue green. It was chiffon and clung, but it swirled. The narrow straps over the shoulders were jeweled, green and blue with an occasional red stone. The neckline was straight, but it was deliberately slanted as if it had been pulled askew by hungry fingers. It was shockingly sexual.

Sally told Amy, "It has a fine Cougar tradition. My Aunt Midge gave it to me, and I'm handing it on to you. Wear it only when you need it. It's foolproof. When you give up the free life, or don't need it any longer, pass it on to another of us. Be selective. No, don't take it off. Keep it on. I want to see Chas as he sees you in that dress."

The dress was a Cougar tradition? Amy knew she couldn't keep it after all. She would have to give it back. But she, too, wanted to see Chas as he saw her in that dress.

Amy decided she would leave it with Chas when she vanished. He could give it back to Sally, and Sally could pass it on to a real cousin. Charlotte? Kate? They wanted it. Connie didn't.

How very interesting it was that Connie didn't want the green dress.

The dress made Amy feel different. More careless. She watched the next film. They were amateurs. Chas was far better. The actors looked silly. That wasn't the way a man made a woman feel. She was a poor actress. Maybe she didn't realize what it was like to really be touched by a man. By Chas. Amy smiled at the green dress and touched one shoulder strap.

Amy and Connie were the only completely sober women when the men arrived to be greeted with delight. Chas saw Amy immediately and his eyes flicked down her and up to her eyes. He didn't even greet her. He asked coldly, "What are you doing in that dress?"

Amy laughed. "Sally gave it to me. It's a Cougar family tradition."

Through his teeth, Chas said, "Take it off. We have to go."

Sally protested from Tad's arms. "Not yet. Wait a while."

Tad laughed. "Let's go, too." And he hugged Sally with great pleasure.

Amy heard Matt ask Connie, "What in hell's the matter with you? Are you in some kind of trouble?"

Connie just shook her head.

Matt urged, "Come on. We have to talk."

"No."

"The hell 'no'! Get a jacket. We're going to walk."

"I can't. I . . . I can't. Leave me alone."

"Is that what you want?"

As Amy was being dragged out of the door, she called back to Sally, "Thanks."

But Sally was watching Chas in a puzzled way. A thoughtful, almost surprised way.

Out on the deck, Chas wrapped his hand around Amy's arm and dragged her along, walking too fast. She protested a little, her breasts bouncing in the soft chiffon as she was forced almost to run. Chas took off his suit coat and draped it around her shoulders, not in tenderness but to cover her. He was acting very oddly.

He didn't speak.

They went down in the elevator to the third floor, he again took her arm as if she would try to escape, and hurried her along to their rooms.

He opened their door, almost shoved her into the bedroom and closed the door. Then through his teeth he said, "Take off that damn dress! Get rid of it!"

He was serious. It wasn't that he wanted her naked, he wanted her out of that dress! "Why?"

"It's a tart's dress."

He was furious! So furious that she tried to soothe him. "It's just a dress."

"It's Sally's! She's a tart, and that's her dress. I don't want you in it. You're not her kind of woman, and I don't want you dressed like a whore. A high-class whore, but one nevertheless."

"I feel pretty in it." Her stubborn resistance to his control was asserting itself.

"She gave it to you deliberately. She wanted me to see you in her dress...she is doing this to try to— Take it off or I'll tear it off." He almost snarled.

"I was going to give it back. I wanted to look beautiful for you."

"You don't need a tart's dress to look beautiful for me. You're beautiful in anything. You'd be just as mind-boggling in a potato sack."

"Thank you."

"I don't want that dress anywhere around you. Give it to me. I'll go take it back now."

With some careful maturity, she told Chas, "I believe you're overreacting."

"Don't kid yourself."

"It makes me think you want Sally."

Then he laughed. His laughter was of surprise and disbelief. He didn't want Sally. Amy was sure of that.

She stood there before him and removed the dress. Then she stood there before him in nothing at all but high heels, his pearl and her pearl earrings.

He looked at her and smiled. He took the dress and wadded it up as he said, "Go bathe and wash your hair. I don't want any taint from this nasty thing on you when I make love with you." Then he said, "I'll be right back."

Amy was thoughtfully drying her hair when Chas returned. He busily came in, stripped, put out his things for the valet service. Then he showered as she glanced around, keeping track of his intrusion into her bath. He opened the curtain and emerged, smiling at her. "Now we're back to how we should be."

Since they were alone, and naked, she assumed he meant to take her to bed instantly. She felt sluggish and overwhelmed with the films and talk and the cigarette smoke in Connie's room. She said, "Chas..."

"Let's go out on the beach and walk in the clean night air."

She smiled up at him. "Perfect!"

They put on their soft sweat suits, their socks and Nikes, and—outside—the air was sweet and invigorating. They didn't take the elevator but went quietly down the deserted stairs and out onto the dark beach.

All was still. The stars were awesome; there was no moon. They didn't talk at first. They walked at a good pace, holding hands, breathing deeply and looking around.

They walked a long way. It was coming back that they began to talk. But she avoided a good deal of the sharing he did. She still planned to leave him. Therefore, she was cautious about returning the information or ideas or opinions he shared so easily with her. She didn't want to know him that well. Yes, she did. But she could leave a stranger much easier than she could leave a friend.

How was she to say goodbye to this man? Her first lover.

They had one surprise. Tad and Sally walked by them, heading away from the hotel. They, too, held hands. Their heads were down as they concentrated on each other, so deep in conversation that they didn't see Amy and Chas.

Amy asked in soft concern, "Second thoughts?"

Chas replied, "No. They aren't quarreling or disagreeing, they're sharing . . . like I am."

She looked at him sharply in the dark. His wordage again. Sally and Tad were sharing—not as "we are" but as "I am."

Chas knew she was withholding herself from him.

"What did Sally say when you returned the dress?"

"I said, 'Here,' and she said, 'I understand.'"

"How did she say it?"

"Like she understood exactly."

Amy flung out her arm. "I don't."

"You don't have to. All's you have to do is obey."

"Now Chas..." But why argue? She would be leaving.

"Would you stay over until Tuesday? I can arrange my schedule so we could have a couple more days here. The suite is available. I checked. We could be by ourselves. Can you?"

A positive reply would throw him off his guard. She could say yes and then he wouldn't watch her so closely. That way, she could get away gracefully.

She'd leave a note—and his pearl—and just leave.

Aloud, she told Chas, "I'm free this week." It was no real answer, no commitment.

"Good. That will give me more time."

She didn't ask for what. She thought she knew. Bedtime. To change the subject she said, "I haven't yet met Bob and...was it Jean?"

Rather blankly he questioned, "Bob and Jean?"

"The cousins who needed your suite."

"Oh, *yes!* Well, you see . . . the kid had measles, after all."

"I thought it was chicken pox."

"It may well have been."

She walked beside him in the starry night with the sound of the Gulf curling nearby. She considered how her attitude had undergone some changes.

She still had to leave, but first, leaving had been because it was only a brief affair, as she preferred. Then, leaving was for his sake. But now she must escape for her own sake.

Ah, and there was another change. The wordage had gone from leave to escape.

Eight

The next morning at eight, Chas's wrist alarm buzzed in Amy's ear. He had to reach across her to turn it off. He said, "My arm's paralyzed because some lazy, worthless woman slept on it all night long, and I can't move it. Therefore that woman will have to sit up, so I can drag my arm off the bed and die a thousand deaths until the damned thing will work again. You're that woman."

"You sure change a lot in just a couple of hours. Last night you were about as sweet as a man can be and . . ."

"In your vast knowledge of men."

"I have come to the sobering conclusion that you're not a morning man."

He rolled over on top of her and glared ferociously into her eyes. "Just because I had to get you so thoroughly petted last night, don't feel so sure about my not being a morning man. I'm an any-time man."

"Oh." She smiled up at him. Then she had to say it, "Your arm seems better."

"It hurts like hell. But there's hurt and endurance, and there's not letting some woman get away with being sassy."

"I see."

"It's a good thing." He rolled off her and held his arm, shaking it and groaning. "I would get tangled up with a cold-footed cuddler."

"I don't recall asking you to envelop me last night. I seem to remember it was you who settled us down and told me to be quiet and go to sleep or you'd wear me out."

"You have a faulty memory. All I tried to do was put my weary bones into bed and sleep. But did you let me? No, you did not. First you make me go out and trudge up and down the damn beach. Then we had to go and soak our bones in the heated pool, and when I finally get up to the rooms, you're hungry and must eat or you'll faint. And when I finally get into bed, your feet are cold. Do you know how many kisses it took to warm them up?"

"How many?"

Chas was appalled! "I thought *you* were counting!"

"No, you make my brain swoon and I can't think."

"Really?" He was like a stroked cat.

"Um-hum."

"But I did get you very thoroughly warm, didn't I." It wasn't a question, it was a smug statement.

"All I remember is that you fed me, finally, then the next thing I knew your alarm woke me up."

"You don't remember my skillful, intricate, exquisite lovemaking?"

"Oh." She was curious, "Did we?"

"I suppose it's best to just give you a utilitarian lesson this morning. You're going to have to work up to my more elaborate ways. Lie still and be quiet. This will be basic."

It was a quarter to nine before the basic was finished, and Chas still had to shower and dress. So he didn't have breakfast before he went to take Connie to the doctor.

"Want me to wait for breakfast?"

"No, we'll take a drive-through order and eat on the way. This might take a while." He leaned and kissed Amy.

"Good luck to her."

"I'll tell her." He paused as he looked at her for a strange minute. Then he smiled at her, a different kind of smile, before he leaned to give her a brief, hurried kiss. And he was gone.

Amy bathed slowly. She was tired. She called room service and ordered a perfect breakfast of eggs, bacon, pancakes, milk, tea and toast with jam. Then she dressed.

With the party the night before, the only Cougars out were the kids. They'd probably been thrown out of their parents' rooms to wear themselves out before the wedding so they'd sit still then. On impulse, Amy went up to Sally's room and tapped with one discreet fingernail. It wouldn't be too loud for someone sleeping, but Sally would hear it if she was awake.

When Sally opened the door, Amy was struck by how different she looked. Amy almost didn't recognize her! Without thinking, Amy said, "You look marvelous!"

"I feel marvelous. We are fitting that miserable dress one more time in just a few minutes. Why not come along and talk to me and keep me company?"

"Sure." Amy agreed to that readily enough, but then she said uncomfortably, "About the green dress..."

"I understand. And, Amy, don't louse up with Chas. He's a special man. Don't be as stupid as the rest of us. Stay the way you are. I believe I don't have to draw any pictures for you. You do understand me?"

Amy simply stared.

Sally went slowly around the room, thinking, then she picked up her white lace veil. "Connie was with me when I got this from our Aunt Karen. It's been in the family forever. We left her place and giggled and laughed and chortled about me wearing a white veil.

"I find, after last night, that my attitude toward this marriage is quite different." She looked up at Amy. "And oddly enough, it was Chas seeing you in that green dress, and being so furious, that started it off.

"Tad and I went out on the beach and talked. We've known each other since college, and we have had no secrets. But after last night, our lives are going to be very different than I thought. We talked about how we look at life and what we want from it, and how we want our children to be. Different from us.

"We are really committed to this marriage. We talked about so many things. Tad and I want the same things. And it was Chas and how he feels about you that opened this all up.

"But, Amy, it was you who made Chas behave in the way he did last night. I've seen him with women and he's always been sure they were treated right, but what they did was their own business. I've never seen him as mad at a woman as he was with you last night. What you do is very important to Chas. I believe he loves you."

"No!"

Sally watched her very seriously. "Be careful of him. He's too good a man to cheat. We are all astonished he moved in with you. There is something very important happening. If you are attracted to him at all, pay attention."

Amy moved restlessly and flung out her arms, "I want a man's life. They have it all. I'm no different. I'm as smart, as innovative. I want to be involved in all the moving and shaping. To sample as I'm attracted. To be—"

Sally interrupted seriously but softly, "To be a damned fool?"

Amy protested, "You say that now. You've had it all!"

"I wish, when I was standing in your shoes all those years ago, someone would have said to me what I'm saying now to you."

Amy frowned. "If your family is anything like mine, they did."

Sally was silent before she said, "They did."

"You might have married years ago and you would never have found Tad. Now you both know what you want. You'll have a good, solid marriage."

"Men rarely marry party girls. At my age women are beginning to realize they don't have a lot of time left to marry and have children. Some don't want children. They'd rather have careers. But most of them want husbands. So they let a man move in with them, in foolish trial marriages.''

Sally then questioned, ''Why should a man marry such a woman? Then the man moves out and marries a younger woman and has children. So the discarded woman—and she does feel discarded—tries another. And another. And marries just to marry if she can find a man who is willing by then. I've seen it. It was looming for me. Sexual freedom is a field day... for men. Pay attention.''

Amy was disgusted. ''Of all people, I wouldn't think you'd be talking this way.''

''There's nothing more convinced than a reformed woman. Listen to me.'' *She* ruffled Amy's hair, then she exclaimed, ''The fitting! We've got to go.''

Amy replied, ''I need to think.''

''Do. That's something I was a long time getting around to doing. I'll see you later.''

They parted outside Sally's door, and Amy saw it was almost eleven. Chas should be back. She needed to look at him. To see him, and not just how he looked. She went to the stairwell and walked down to the third floor. Surely a woman could live like a man. It just took discretion and style. It didn't have to be tawdry or public. It could be done with flair. It depended on the woman.

She dawdled along the third-floor balcony above the garage access, and eventually saw Chas and Connie coming from the parking area. Connie? It *was* Connie! She glowed!

It was as if God had put a funnel in her ear and poured in a gallon of sunshine and the light had flowed like honey through her body to imbue every nerve and cell, even down to the ends of her hair! Incredible! Amy simply stared.

Like two of the fabled gods, Chas and Connie spotted Amy and waved to her with big, bright smiles. And Matt was running toward them. He ignored Chas to take Connie's shoulders in his hands and shake her a little. Since sound rises, Amy heard him demand of her, "Where did you go? What have you been doing?"

Chas split off past them to come to stand two floors below Amy. He said softly, "It's okay. Come down. I'll meet you on the stairs."

Amy glanced again at Matt and Connie. Connie was relaxed and smiling gently, but she was shaking her head. Matt was arguing with her, angry, demanding replies. She did answer, but her manner was very calm. Matt's gestures were wide and he was talking through his teeth. Connie was unperturbed. Frowning, Amy turned toward the stairwell, but Chas was already there. She asked him, "What happened?"

"A rare allergy to her depilatory on very sensitive tissue. Something she never had trouble with before. A fluke, but a painful rash."

"And she's all right?"

"Fine. They ran tests to be sure. And they've made her comfortable. The doctor was an older man, who still believes in Saturday appointments and house calls, and he also believes in lectures." Chas paused and grinned. "He included me." That made him laugh. He was so amused and talkative that he'd obviously been very worried about his cousin, and he was relieved for her.

Amy exclaimed, "All that worry! Over nothing?"

"Ah, but, Amy, it was possible. She had cause. I believe she's reformed."

"I'm surrounded!" Amy retorted petulantly. "Who else is reformed? I'm not."

"You wouldn't be! But Sally is!"

"Who? Sally? Our cousin, Sally? You josh!"

"Yes. She is!"

"That wouldn't just be a reformation, it would be a transformation!"

"She gave me a lecture."

"I'd give an eyetooth to have heard *that!*" His tone scoffed.

"She told me you are a good man."

His green eyes came to her blue ones suddenly serious. "She told you that? She's on my side in this?"

"In what?"

"Uh . . . you may not have noticed, Amy, but I'm attracted to you."

Without concealing her impatience, she informed him, "You first saw me Thursday morning on the beach. This is Saturday morning. That is two days' time. This is a brief interlude. It would never have happened if you *hadn't* been attracted. It has no other meaning.

"This is a very micro period in our lives. I leave to . . . Tuesday." She'd almost said "tomorrow." "We'll go our separate ways. I've told you my life is such that I can't include any meetings or continue this acquaintance."

"Acquaintance? You call *this* an acquaintance? What do you call a relationship?"

"Something a lot longer in time, with some mutual regard."

"Our regard is mutual."

She looked at him almost painfully as she admitted, "You are a special man. I'm glad you're my first." Her eyes were sad and her tone worse.

He touched her cheek and his voice was reedy as he told her, "We'll talk about this on Monday when everyone is gone and we've had a decent night's sleep. When there are no crises to distract us."

With sad deliberation, she agreed, "Monday should solve everything." She thought she was being clever with her honest wordage, and those words would stop any more arguments.

How could she stay? She was there under false pretenses. She would have to go away from there and leave Chas forever. To avoid continuing on that difficult subject, Amy then said, "I must buy a gift for Sally and Tad."

"You're giving all of us the gift of you as a new cousin. That's enough."

She blushed with guilt. "I need to find a gift."

"I've included you on mine. I got them a silver punch bowl with tray and twenty-four silver cups. Cougars entertain quite a bit. Her older sister gets the family one, so Sally will have to have another. We've solved that."

"Do you entertain a lot?"

"Yes. Business. Family. I have some very good friends. You will like them, and they'll go a little berserk over you. They'll think you're a princess I've snared with golden apples and a unicorn."

Chas thought he'd snared her? He still didn't even suspect she'd set up this whole seduction? He was an innocent. He may have tried a woman or two, but basically he was an innocent.

If he felt that way, in leaving him she would hurt him. Why couldn't he be more experienced so they could just enjoy this holiday? Laugh over her trickery? And part with cheery goodbyes? It was his possessive attitude that was making her so miserable over leaving.

He said, "You treat me differently than a woman treats a man."

Amy asked, "How?"

Chas considered before he said, "More as an... equal, or a friend."

"I am your equal. And I have been friendly."

He inquired, "How equal?"

"Whatever you can do in the business world, I can equal it in some way. Of course that's if you are management. I can't chop down as many trees in a day, but I probably could chop enough down to keep a house warm, given enough time for it."

Chas was charmed. "Competitive little rascal."

"Not competitive as much as equal. There is a difference. I don't want to stand in your place, I want to stand beside you with equal authority."

His voice gentle, Chas told her, "Any good businessman knows someone must take command. Defused authority confuses. Power struggles weaken and disperse authority. Equality is a very difficult thing to actually achieve, even for a man. For a young and pretty woman, it's damned near impossible. How important is your career?"

"I find it fascinating. However, it's always a struggle until the men I work with take me seriously. Or will at least listen to what I say without seeing me first as a woman."

"I'm not sure there's much hope for change there. Men first see women as women. No one denies women have that handicap in business. But eventually, if the woman is skilled, men will see the skill next."

Amy said, "You admit that."

"I'm honest. I've told you so, and I will never lie to you."

She looked away from him, out over the complex. Her heart bore the weight of her own lie. She saw no way to mend it.

Quite gently he said, "I'm starved. Come, let's eat."

Amy decided the gloom that settled over her was from having so little sleep. These last few days had been quite different from anything she'd ever experienced.

In all her life, she had never been involved with so many people for such an extended period of time. The stories and connections, the problems and quarrels, the hilarity and sheer weight of words were almost overwhelming.

And then there was Chas.

In her, he had wakened and sated hungers that she'd never known existed. And the lassitude of her body was different. The awareness of it was unusual. There was the almost driving need to be close to him, to touch him even in public. To have a hand on his arm. To feel his voice inside her chest in a strange way.

In such a short time, she had heard too much, witnessed too much and felt too much. She was exhausted from her uncharted voyage into the emotional experience of being a part of something so extraordinary. And then there was not only her awareness of Chas, but there was her feeling for him.

It was frivolous to suspect her feeling for him could be anything close to actual love. Love never happened in such a short time. She'd known him, been *aware* of him, only since she registered in the lobby just three days ago, on Wednesday night.

But look at all that had happened in that short time! It was almost as if she'd had a complex seminar on family ties and sexual conduct in a weirdly condensed time warp, with the minutes folded back on themselves and packed tightly with more than enough alien experience.

Perhaps people *could* learn a foreign language in one week. She'd never believed it possible. It would only depend on how it was offered. Like the Short, Comprehensive Cougar Seminar in Familial Relationships.

And then there was Chas with his expertise. She had been so grateful he had been her first. Perhaps she was wrong in that gratitude. Perhaps if she'd had someone not quite so superior, so skilled, so attractive, this experience wouldn't be turning so painful.

Ah. So. Amy was now admitting that it wasn't Chas's pain that occupied her concern, it was her own. She would hate to leave him. She was anguished with the thought of never seeing him again. How had she ever gotten into this fix? Affairs were light, delightful, titillating fun. What had gone wrong?

It had started with a lie. Without that lie, she might salvage something from this in just knowing Chas. Even if she didn't continue the affair, she would like to know him and what happened to him. Whom he married. What his kids would be like. How they would look. If his wife liked him.

"What's the matter?"

"What?"

"You're not eating. And now you have tears on your cheeks. What's wrong?"

She smiled and straightened. Then she used that same excuse again. Only this time it was true. "I'm a little overwhelmed by your family. I've never been around so many people. I had worried about Connie, and I'm so relieved she's okay. I'm worn out with all the emotion."

"We'll go up and take a nap."

"I believe I'd like to be alone for a while."

"You go up and take a nap. I'll see how I can be helpful for tonight's arrangements."

"Thank you, Chas." She felt awkward. "It isn't that I don't want to be with you or..."

"I do understand." He touched her hand. "I'll come up in a couple of hours to waken you, so you'll be ready in time for the wedding. Take a good deep bath, but don't go to sleep in the tub."

She smiled. "I won't." He kissed her. She smiled up at him again and said, "Goodbye."

After they'd separated, she walked along to the elevator, thinking how odd it had been for her to say goodbye that way. Suddenly she *knew* she had to leave *then*.

The goodbye may have been her subconscious telling her to go and leave, nothing could be gained by staying any longer. If she stayed even another day, her heart could be so entangled with foolish love for Chas that she'd really suffer.

Wasn't she suffering now?

Yes, but another day would make it that much worse. She went to their suite, figured up her half of the bill and put the cash on the table.

Then Amy sat down and wrote a note. She wrote ten notes. She used two pages with all the crossed scratches each page could endure, and she labored over the words so that she got a dreadful headache.

She finally made do with:

Goodbye. I must confess I'm no kin at all. My grandmother's name wasn't Winsome. I'm sorry I used you so crassly. I hope I haven't ruined your opinion of all women. There are some very fine women. You're a fine man, and the woman who marries you will be very, very fortunate!

After some frustrated anguishing, she again wrote:

Goodbye.

She read it over several times, not really paying any attention. She was exhausted emotionally and not too well organized. She added:

Please tell Sally I was called away. Thank you.

She refrained from writing yet another goodbye.

It was no trick at all to pack. She had kept things quite organized. That was probably a good thing, considering the state she was in. So she gathered what was hers, cast long, sad glances at his things, and she ran a lingering hand slowly over his jacket sleeve. She put her door card with the note and money, and she left.

Remarkably, she encountered no one. Of course, she sneaked downstairs, took the hidden walks and went through the most obscure halls, out to the other side of the buildings and to her car. She got in and drove away.

It was over.

Her first affair was over. She wished she'd never launched herself on such a stupid, hurtful thing. It wasn't as attractive as she thought it would be. It wasn't all fun. Affairs weren't casual. They were a serious undertaking that interfered with other lives.

She had been a fool.

She took Highway 275 to 4 and drove east to Winter Haven. The highway was a good one, and she drove carefully, but her thoughts roiled along.

She understood she wasn't cut out for affairs. She'd made the biggest mistake of her life, and she would never see Chas again. She could never match him with another man. And she was extraordinarily unhappy.

She wanted to crawl into a hole and pull the ground in after her so she could be alone and endure as she grieved for the loss of him.

She thought: I am different. I'm a woman. I don't want to be a man.

Nine

Amy had already driven into the home driveway, and gotten out of her car. She realized her parents were there at the poolside table with other people. With an irritating shock, Amy saw the Peckerels were still visiting.

She was trapped. Flight was out of the question. There was no cordial way she could leave at that point.

Her smiling mother was already on her feet, and her father was coming toward her with a great, welcoming grin.

Amy stretched her lips when what she wanted to do was fling herself against her father's wide chest and just bawl. It wasn't the Peckerels' fault they didn't know they weren't supposed to be there right then.

Bill Allen tousled his daughter's hair in welcome and gave her a buffeting hug. Then with his heavy arm around her weakened, drooping shoulders, he turned her toward her approaching mother.

With great smothered hilarity, her mother exclaimed, "How nice you could get here in time to see the Peckerels!"

Amy managed a cold glance before she stretched her mouth into some semblance of a smile and said, "Yes." With that quite sketchy acknowledgment to her maternal parent, she went on to the group and held out her hand as she said, "Mitzie! I did get here in time. How are you? Obviously perfect."

Mitzie rose and even leaned a cheek almost close enough for a belatedly offered air-kiss and she replied, "Uh..."

Amy did wait encouragingly, but Mitzie had forgotten what it was she was going to say. Amy smiled and shook hands with Peck, who jerked her heartily to him and gave her a juicy smack on her cheek.

It was then Amy saw who else was there. A very amused man. He'd risen, and her eyes followed him up. He was perfect.

His name was Miles Clifford. He was big, he was easy, he was perfect. His eyes danced and his mouth's smile kept—almost—slipping out of control. He liked her. This was the man her mother had found for her to marry. He was too late. She looked at him gloomily.

Her mother touched Amy's arm and said to the others, "We'll be back in just a minute. I know Amy would like to freshen up."

While her father retrieved the designated suitcase, her mother led her daughter's faltering steps to the house, inside and up the stairs.

After her father had heartily deposited the case in Amy's room and departed, her mother asked, "What's wrong?"

Amy said simply, "My life's over." She flung out both arms and flopped back onto the bed to lie flat, staring at the ceiling.

"A man," Cynthia Allen guessed.

Amy managed a single nod.

"Married?"

One shake.

"Well, he would have to be interested in our daughter, the man killer, so what's the problem?"

"I lied to him."

"Well, a fib now and again—"

Without moving her head, Amy moved her eyes over to her mother in a quelling way. "When he finds out the truth, he'll never speak to me again."

"Tell me."

It was like doing a lousy job of pulling a champagne cork, and the entire story was out of Amy in a fizzing of words, tears and lamentations.

Cynthia only interrupted once, and that was to exclaim, "Trilby? Trilby *Winsome?*"

Amy's irritated, "Yes!" was patched into the edge of her rush of words. Amy didn't tell *everything*. She censored the fact that she'd spent almost thirty-six hours, all told, intimately, with Chas.

Even though she was only a pretend "cousin," she found she couldn't be harsh about Sally or Connie, so she didn't tell that part or mention the green dress. Without all that, it actually shouldn't have taken very long to tell her story of deception.

It took a while.

She had to make her mother understand how marvelous Chas was, and she'd botched her single chance for happiness through her carelessness. He was an honest man who couldn't tolerate cheaters or liars, and she was both.

Her whole lying career had been condensed into those two and a half days, and she'd never tell another lie in all the rest of her life. Her bleak, loveless life was finished. She was going to go and nurse the lepers.

"Yes." Cynthia had to agree, and she even managed a sympathetic sounding sigh. "But first we have to go down and be civil to the Peckerels ... and to Miles. He's such a dear. Come along. Have you something in this case, or should your father bring up the rest of it?"

"This one," Amy said dispiritedly, as she dragged herself off the bed, picked the case up from the floor, and flopped it onto the bed. She pressed the locks and opened it. Then she rooted around for shoes and ... pulled out a handful of ... business cards? She looked at them with a frown. They belonged to *Chas!* She burst into tears.

There must have been two hundred of his cards tucked into every corner of her case, between folds of her clothing, in her shoes, everywhere! When had he put them there? How dare he to think she would sneak away? How could he do this to her? She flung herself into her mother's arms and sobbed. Cynthia hugged her close, and she smiled.

After a shower rinse, and cold compresses for her eyes, careful makeup and a sugared glass of lemonade, Amy joined the others outside. She was very quiet. Miles was attentive, but not too. Everyone's conversation went right over Amy's head. She sat in a vacuum.

Cynthia took up the conversational slack, replying for Amy in such a way that Amy could nod or shake her head. Then Miles took it up. After giving his own opinion, he'd add enough information for her to comment, and his eyes would rest on her thoughtfully.

Since Bill never bothered with details, he was oblivious to his daughter's behavior. Peck had never advanced from his experiences in Vietnam, so something current wasn't important; and Mitzie was concerned only with herself.

Mitzie was a thrift shop copy of a courtesan. She didn't move her face at all. To smile she opened her mouth a little. She was conscious of her every movement and did each one just so. Then she would check to see if the male was aware of her. She moved now for Miles's appreciation.

A true courtesan isn't blatant. She only wants to please a man. She works with humor, or questions, or as a listener. She works with enticement, if that's what he wants, and she has skill in bed. Mitzie couldn't do those things. Mitzie didn't flirt or tempt as much as she simply was there to be admired.

Miles glanced at Mitzie enough to let her feel she was appreciated. Bill was unaware. Cynthia shared the knowledge of Mitzie with Miles, and they understood that Peck watched indulgently.

Some men like their women to attract other men, just as long as that's all that comes of it. It makes such men feel they have a prize. So they don't mind a little—distant—flirting. Peck was like that.

Catching Cynthia's eye, Miles then tilted his head at Amy and raised questioning brows. Her mother shrugged minutely. Miles then set himself to draw Amy out of her shell. He was charming.

Of course, Miles also had to stay aware of Mitzie. In their little group, Mitzie wasn't part of the conversation, so her only entertainment was moving for Miles. If he ignored her, she would sink into boredom. So he gave her enough glances, but he concentrated his attention on Amy.

Amy did reply. She roused herself and said words and even focused on Miles, now and then, with some bitterness.

He really was perfect. He wasn't at all like Chas. He was treating her like a whole person, an equal. Not like Chas, who was domineering and dictatorial. Miles was far superior. She could tell just by looking at him.

How could her guardian angel have allowed her to get into such a mess down at the Cougar gathering? Why hadn't the warning bells sounded and... They had.

Amy distinctly remembered hearing them and realizing they had sounded all along throughout her life and prevented just such a thing, as had happened, from ever happening before then. Why then? How disastrous.

Mitzie stood up slowly, carefully straightened her skirt, slid it up just a little to allow some give for her shapely hips and sat again. As they should have, they all watched Mitzie do that.

Miles got to hear how Peck saved Bill's life and was duly impressed. Bill laughed. He enjoyed Peck's gradual changing of history. Obviously they should all thank God—now—that Peck had been in Vietnam or it would have been another Korea, to hear Peck tell it.

Bill rubbed his nose and coughed a little, but he never demurred.

Miles was attentive—he'd heard war stories before.

Peck looked indulgently complacent with self-worth. Cynthia smiled. Mitzie slowly crossed her knees with a studied tucking of her short skirt, and Amy was lost to her own thoughts.

She was thinking that, by then, Chas would have had some succinct questions for Peck. He would have slid them in nicely and tightened the loop just enough to make Peck uncertain, but Chas wouldn't have "killed" the story. He would have just made Peck give a more honest version. Yes. Chas wouldn't allow out-and-out lies. What had she done?

Right then, Chas was up in their room finding her note and the pearl . . . *She was still wearing his pearl!* My God! She was a fallen women! She'd kept his gift! Where had her wits been when she wrote that stupid note? That cool goodbye? No woman was worth the cost of that pearl! But she'd taken it along. She had!

She had his card. She had more than enough of his cards. She would return the pearl by special courier. She must. She touched it there on her chest. How could she give it up? She could have it appraised, send him the money by special messenger—anonymously, of course—and keep the pearl as a memento. As a token of their . . . coming together. Ahh . . .

"How about you, Amy," Miles was saying to her. "Do you gorge yourself on orange juice down here?"

She was being swept into another titillating Peck-erel conversation. She nodded. And Mitzie volunteered, "I love orange juice."

They all smiled at her, and she modestly straightened her shoulder strap as she peeked at Miles.

Peck added confidingly, "It makes my bowels run."

Cynthia hastily commented, "I've never seen the bougainvillea so vigorous as this year. I just found it's a member of the Four o'clock family. Did you ever make chains from Four o'clocks?"

Miles said, "I don't believe I ever have."

Cynthia's eyes twinkled at Miles. "Since they're called Four o'clocks, because they are an evening flower, I was somewhat disappointed they would open earlier. My mother told me it was daylight savings that threw their timing off."

A stimulating day. The evening didn't improve. They continued in their individual ways, Bill trying to discuss Central America and the political fields in the United States, Mitzie rearranging her clothes or position. Cynthia was working for a cohesive conversation with Miles's help and then there was the lump called Amy.

The wedding would have begun. Sally and Tad. What about Connie and Matt? All those lives Amy's had touched, and she would never know what happened to them. Or Chas. What would happen to Chas?

When she found herself in the kitchen helping to get the meal on the table, Amy listened as her mother was saying, "It would have been interesting to see how other children would have been. You're fascinating. But do try to help with the table talk. Just for that time, then you can sink back into your black abyss for the rest of the evening. Then you will rest up for tomorrow. Miles is here for the weekend. You need to be courteous. I am a little embarrassed by your conduct."

Amy turned indignant eyes to her abnormal mother. "I would certainly hate to embarrass you!" Amy puffed. "All's *I* have to cope with is the disastrous ruining of my entire life and you want me to make... *table conversation?*"

"Please." Cynthia responded rather coolly.

"Good grief."

"A lady can handle anything," Cynthia reminded her. "You are not to make our guests uncomfortable."

"What about me?"

"Later."

They stared at each other. Amy was especially annoyed that her mother was right. One could not allow self-indulgence. One straightened one's spine and coped. She would survive. Even this.

Even never seeing Chas again in all the rest of her life, she would learn to cope, to endure, to contribute. That's how people managed. And it was all part of the rules of living. Like behaving, telling the truth and coping. Although somewhat stiff, she said to her mother, "I beg your pardon."

"Ah. I do love you."

"I can't handle mushy right now."

"Neither can I."

They worked in silence. Then Cynthia said, "How sad to sit at the table for dinner. Mitzie loses half her allure."

Laughter erupted from Amy, and she laughed too much. But mother and daughter quickly hugged, then parted, wiped their eyes, washed their hands, patted cool water on their faces, and served the meal.

And Amy did cope. She was attentive, if a little pale, and she contributed. Miles's eyes watched her. He was very aware and quite curious.

Being half-concealed by the table didn't hamper Mitzie. She could squirm in her chair, adjust her shoulder straps slowly and she could lick her lips.

Peckerel expansively told Bill what Congress should do about Central Africa. And how the United Nations should handle it without fooling around.

Amy knew Chas would then ask hard questions, and he'd wait—not helping—for Peck to figure it out. Chas would feel anyone was responsible for his views and should be able to explain them and justify them. On the other hand, Miles just listened politely and made no comment.

Cynthia asked Miles, "Is there any way you could stay through this next week?" and they exchanged a long glance.

He thoughtfully bit into his bottom lip and squinted his eyes at Amy's mother before he replied, "I'll check it out."

Cynthia understood and nodded.

Amy, too, understood. Her mother meant to give her time to know how perfect Miles was. She knew it already. It didn't make any difference.

A week in Miles's company wouldn't prove anything. Nothing except that Amy had been an idiot to ever get involved with someone so hard-nosed as Chas Cougar. He was domineering, possessive, dictatorial and imperfect.

Eventually the evening ended, the assorted people separated in the upper hall, and they went to their own rooms and closed doors. Amy was alone. For the first time since Thursday morning, Amy was alone. Alone.

It was bad enough in a group and suffering; it was hell being alone with her anguish. She would never see Chas again.

She was sitting like a lump on her bedside when there was a quiet tap on her door. Miles? Her career was begun. Did Miles know that? Was her look now that of a woman who sneaked around halls in the night and welcomed strange men into her bed? Was she marked with the look of a loose woman for the rest of her life?

The tap came again, softer. She looked at the door. If she had really become a bedhopper, she would go to the door and smile up at him. She might not let him in—this first night—but she wouldn't discourage him. And if she simply couldn't, this soon after a man like Chas, she would be kinder in her refusal than she used to be. Much, much kinder.

But she wasn't a bedhopper. She wasn't a pseudo man. She was a woman, and she didn't want to end up like Connie, Sally, Kate or Charlotte. Or, as Sally had told Connie, meet a man whom she didn't recognize even though she had spent a weekend with him. Amy knew she would never again allow a casual affair. It was too stupid.

Actually, as much as she grieved for Chas, she was fortunate she had had her affair with him. He could have been crude or embarrassing. Chas was none of those things. He was a gentleman. She wished ... She wis—

To her astonishment, the knob on her door turned and the door began to open. Miles was shockingly persistent! How could he come into her room the first night in her father's house?

And her mother came into the room.

"Mother." Amy was blank.

Cynthia agreed. "Daughter." And she looked at said daughter quizzically. "Are you all right?"

"As I will ever be." Amy was mournful.

"I do appreciate you rallying tonight. Hop into bed and get a good night's sleep. Tomorrow will be better."

"Mother," Amy retorted from a more knowledgeable height. "There are things in this life that a good night's sleep will not solve."

"Not too much."

"You were very fortunate to meet a man who was tolerant of you and allowed you to call the shots."

"He wasn't at all tolerant. There were times he was bloody mad." Cynthia lifted her brows and smiled.

"You lived in another time."

"For God's sake, Amy, don't be so narrow-minded to tell me Times Are Different. That wail is in *every* generation from Adam and Eve. Now *they* could say it! You can't. Morals and manners are constant. So is the keeping and flaunting of rules."

"Morals are relaxed now."

"My mother was too young for World War Two. But at that time it was war that was the Great Excuse. Don't be so naive as to think anything is ever different."

"People accept living together."

"Some do. Even that isn't unique."

"Mom, I have a dreadful headache. I really can't debate this tonight."

"Ah, my dear. I would never have you sad."

"My life is over."

"Surely you're not so poor spirited that you would turn up your toes and quit?"

"I need time to grieve."

Cynthia gave her a patient look. "If you must. But it seems to me excessive for a two-day acquaintance?"

"We...made...love."

"Oh?" Cynthia tilted her head and pushed up her lower lip. "He must have made quite an...impression."

Amy shot a quick look at her mother, but her face was bland. Amy said, "I'm as good as any man. They have casual affairs." That sounded...adolescent.

"Not that many do."

"I can have any kind of life I want." Amy wasn't as sure now.

"But why be a man? You are a woman. There are all the marvels of being an orange. Why try to be an apple? Men are marvelous! They are so different from us. They are so unique. Their thinking is amazing. Their interests. Why in the world would you be a cat trying to swim upstream with salmon?"

"How nice you are contented and so glad to be a woman."

"Not always. The problems facing you are faced by most women somewhere along the way. If you find this...Chas? so remarkable, why don't you mend your foolishness? Why not go to him and be honest about what you've done?"

"You don't know Chas." Amy grieved. "He's such an honest man. He told me—how many times—that he never lies. I lied. I did it on impulse!

"Good Lord, Mother, don't *ever* tell Daddy I did anything so impulsive and stupid! He thinks I'm levelheaded. It would disillusion him. I would hate to disappoint him that badly."

"And yourself? Have you disappointed yourself? Is that what's really bothering you? You've broken some very sound rules. But, Amy, they can be glued back together. Rules are for a reason. This is an example."

"You're a good woman."

Her mother replied gently, "So are you."

Amy was incredulous. "You can say that? After this mad conduct?"

"One slip does not a fallen woman make. The fact that you are suffering is a mark of your character. You don't justify what you did. You're ashamed of lying. You'll come around. You'll survive this. You'll be stronger."

Amy grieved. "I'm not quite ready to accept the fact that you could be right."

"None of us ever is. When we live, in that space of time, we are the ones who know it all." Cynthia advised. "Don't waste time with regrets. Straighten your spine and go on."

"In a while."

"Ah, yes. The grieving." Cynthia moved to walk a pace or two, then turned again to look at Amy. "Must you grieve?"

"He's worth it."

"Then go to him and tell him so."

"He'd slam the door in my face."

"Maybe not. At least you would have tried. And he might admire guts."

"Like Daddy, he has a code."

"If he's really like your father, his code is hardest on himself, but he understands not everyone can live up to his standards."

"Chas deserves a woman who can."

"Wow! You have a full-blown crush on him, haven't you?"

"Is that it? It couldn't be love this soon, could it? I could recover from a crush."

Cynthia mentioned, "Miles is a special man. He might be the Alka-Seltzer that will cure you of Chas."

"What a romantic parallel." Amy was still sitting on the side of the bed. "Treat a lost love like an upset stomach?"

Cynthia agreed, "Most of life is Tums."

"I wouldn't trade you for any other mother."

"Then I've been much too lenient."

Amy nodded. "Probably. But I do like you."

"Oh, Amy." They looked at each other, both teary-eyed, then Cynthia leaned down and hugged her daughter. "Good night, my love. Sleep."

"...perchance to dream?" Amy's tears spilled over onto her cheeks.

"If it helps."

Amy was so exhausted that she did sleep. And she did dream. She dreamed Chas was *furious!* He looked like a bear seriously challenging another in that head forward, threatening way that is very intimidating. He snarled, "And just why did you take off that way?"

Amy had learned over the years—what with one thing or another—that when someone asks such a question, in that way, they don't really want an actual answer. What they want is to vent their spleen and, no matter what the reply, the questioner will be angrier.

That's exactly why children say, "I don't know." It's short. It is a reply. And the phrase is so maddening that it distracts the questioner from the original problem.

That was the dream. The nightmares were another thing. In those she went up to Chas in a crowded room and touched his arm to get his attention. He turned and grinned down at her. She realized he wasn't angry, and she raised her mouth for his kiss.

The dream Chas responded magnificently. Her toes curled in the cramped toes of her high-heeled shoes, her knees dissolved and her body hunger concentrated. He lifted his mouth from the kiss and smiled at her. Then he put his arm around her and held her close to his side as people intruded for his attention.

As happens in dreams, Amy couldn't understand their words, but everyone seemed laughing and friendly. She was the only stranger. They ignored her, talking to Chas, and finally Chas asked low in her ear, "What's your name?"

In the nightmare, Chas had forgotten her. When every cell in her body knew him, yearned for him, he had forgotten her. Like his cousin, Sally, he'd forgotten a bed partner.

The Cougars must prowl and forget. She hadn't meant a thing to him. She was just another willing woman. It was devastating.

She wakened to small, weeping gasps, wet cheeks and depression. It was only a dream.

But dreams are sometimes portents. She would remember him all the rest of her life. Would Chas forget her? Or would he only remember that she'd ducked out on him? How sad.

She dragged out of bed the next morning, unrested, gloomy, not giving one hoot if the Peckerels were present or not, or even Miles. She didn't even care about how awkward it would be for her parents if she languished in her room and didn't appear.

The only thing that pried her out from her bed was training. She was supposed to do her share, so she got up. In all of history, no Allen had ever let anyone down.

She had. She had deserted Chas and left him alone to make her excuses at the wedding. How embarrassing for him. He could handle it. He was the most capable man she'd ever met. He was the one everyone turned to. Why wasn't he here to comfort her? She needed him.

It was Sunday. She pulled on neat gray cotton slacks with a red cotton pullover and stared at herself in the mirror. No man could ever be entranced by such a lump. She brushed her limp hair and dragged her feet down to breakfast. She wasn't hungry.

Their slender, middle-aged cook looked up from the morning paper and said, "Anytime," in a sour way.

"Hello to you, too," Amy replied with equal hostility.

"Be careful how you speak to me. If I quit, and your mother starts cooking, Bill will have your hide."

"I love you, Lucy." Amy said it as if automated.

"Equally." Lucy didn't move but sat studying Amy. "What the hell's happened to you?"

"Thank God Dad's not in the diplomatic corps." Amy got up and put bread in the toaster and poured herself a cup of coffee.

"Only a man could wreak such havoc. Who is he?"

Amy retorted, "None of your damned business."

"Ah, baby, is it hopeless?"

"Don't go mushy on me, Lucy, I can't handle it."

"So. The rat." She got up from the chair and opened the refrigerator. "Coddled eggs."

"I'll gag."

"You have to put something under that coffee or you'll ruin the lining of your stomach."

"It's my stomach."

"Since I'm the cook here, if your stomach is ruined, it reflects on me—therefore you will protect my reputation, or I'll sue."

"So sue."

Lucy turned at the stove to look at Amy again. "That bad, huh?"

Amy gave her a level stare. "Yes. Where are the parents?"

"They took the Peckerels to church, then to brunch. They'll be gone until two or three o'clock. As soon as I feed you and Tarzan, I'll be leaving."

"T-Tarzan?"

"Miles Clifford. He's in the pool." Lucy hesitated, then asked softly, "Who did you think?"

Amy shook her head. "No one." Amy had been peripherally aware of motion in the pool, across the terrace. Now she looked out through the window bank, across the bricked, tree-shaded terrace, to the pool and saw Miles swimming effortlessly in laps. He swam well.

"That's some man out there." Lucy's voice was sexy. "I couldn't take my eyes off him. Too bad he doesn't just stand around out there in a little bitty fig leaf."

"You're a shocking woman." Amy had told Lucy that before. It was a rote reply.

But about then Miles reached the end of the pool, braced his hands on the edge and effortlessly lifted himself from the water. He was some man. Beautiful. Like Chas.

"Umm."

"Lucy! Don't burn the eggs."

"I'll bet he'll be hungry." Lucy chuckled softly.

Since her sojourn with Chas, Amy had a wider knowledge of innuendo. She now understood the facets of meanings to ordinary words. She blushed.

Lucy watched her blush with great interest before she said with drawling emphasis, "I was talking about food."

"The eggs!" Amy's tone was a little hostile.

Lucy went to the terrace door and called, "Don't bother to dress. Just put on your robe, breakfast is ready."

It wasn't. Lucy obviously wanted to have Miles at the table that way. Mostly naked. He would have to sit there a long time, in that toweling robe, while Lucy fixed his breakfast. She was a lecherous old lady. Or did she think Miles would distract Amy?

Ten

Amy watched as, out by the pool, Miles toweled off and vigorously rubbed his hair almost dry. He was magnificent, although not quite the bulk of Chas. Did Miles realize he was gorgeously made? He pulled on the terry robe, and combed his hair with careless fingers. He wasn't vain.

He came to the kitchen door, and his pupils widened as he saw Amy sitting there at the table. He was attracted to her. He grinned as he walked to the chair across from her, and he said, "Good morning!" as he sat down.

She replied a subdued, "G'morning." Her thoughts had sunk down to sublevel. Here she was at the breakfast table with the man her mother had found for her, and she couldn't dredge up a smile or a sparkle or even an interest. All because of that impulse to meet Chas.

If she hadn't been so rash—and ruined her entire life—she would now be mildly flirting with this superior man. She would be taking up Lucy's bits of conversation and making Miles laugh.

He'd said something to Amy. Amy asked, "What?"

"The pool is perfect."

"We all swim." Amy knew that Miles was ideal. He would fit right in. Bill would be comfortable with him, Cynthia would adore him and Amy would have been contented all the rest of her life.

Miles said, " 'Bye, Lucy."

Lucy was leaving. Amy's parents and the Peckerels would be gone for several hours. She and Miles were going to be there, alone, in the house. All that time, just the two of them. If she was the man-izer she'd hoped to be, it would be the opportunity to taste her second superior male. Amy sighed forlornly.

"Who is he?"

Amy lifted her lashes and gave Miles a blank look.

He elaborated, "The man who keeps you from hearing me. Who is he?"

"Yes. Well, you see... It could have been such fun. I just thought— You're a man. You know how it is. I never dreamed—"

"So that *is* the problem. There is a man."

"Well, actually, no. I met... I decided..." Then she blurted, "How did you recover from your first affair?" She waited with all her attention concentrated on him.

"Ah. This is going to take some time. Let's put the dishes in the sink, and you can come upstairs and watch me pack, while I listen."

"You're leaving?"

"Yes. I've told your parents goodbye. I waited until you surfaced before I left."

Absentmindedly, Amy helped with the dishes, then trailed along upstairs to his room. She asked, "How old were you?"

"When?" Miles began to pack. He was walking back and forth, carrying things to his suitcases.

"With your first affair."

He asked, "What makes you think I ever had one?"

"You're a man," Amy explained.

"And you believe all men concentrate solely on bedding women?"

"To my knowledge." She clarified her question.

Miles was sure. "Not all."

"I don't believe you."

He was polite. "You're a victim of sexism."

"Then you've never had an affair?"

"Why does that have anything to do with your problem?"

"I need to know what to do to recover."

He was kind. "Take it one day at a time."

"That's...all?"

"How does anyone get past anything?" He chose slacks, a shirt and underwear.

Amy grieved. "This seems too devastating for so simple a solution."

Bluntly, Miles said, "So was Hiroshima."

"You mock me," Amy chided. "One love affair can't compare to Hiroshima."

"No. But they, too, recovered. So in comparison, you can."

He went to take a shower then, and she sat in his room and looked, unseeing, out the window. He was probably right. She would manage. Ah, Chas.

Miles came back, dressed, still toweling his hair. "Your eyes are focused on me!"

"You're a very nice man."

"Not good enough." He began to pack.

"I thought you were going to stay the week."

"I said I'd check things out. I can't stay, now." He gave her a weighing look. "But I'd like to come back in a couple of months and see you again."

Although she said, "Yes," it wasn't a strong reply.

"I'll be back." He zipped the bags closed and put them by the door. "You'll be here this summer?"

"It'll depend. I travel."

"We might meet. I'll check your schedule." He reached into his wallet. "Here's my number. When..." He looked up as he handed her the card, so he saw her stricken look.

Chas had put all those cards in her suitcase. Did men do that all the time? Amy thought of that as she reached out an automatic hand and took Miles's card.

"He gave you his card?" He stated what was obvious.

"Yes."

"Then he must be sure you'll call him. You might do that." Miles's words were reluctant even to his own ears. He wasn't sure if he wanted to encourage her to get in touch with any other man.

"It isn't an ordinary circumstance. I... was under false colors. I gave another name."

"I see." He smiled. Perhaps she'd boxed herself in quite neatly and whoever the other man was he would be out of the picture. Miles was very tempted to stay, but all she could think of, right then, was that other man. When Miles was with Amy, he wanted her attention on him.

It was smarter for him to leave. When he saw her again, his being coupled in her mind with the other incident wouldn't be so strong.

If he listened to her now, later she would feel he knew too much about her. Their relationship wouldn't begin as it should. This way was better. "It was great to meet you, and I'll... anticipate the next time." He picked up the cases and waited.

"You're leaving now." Amy confirmed the obvious.

"It's been very nice. Your parents are remarkable."

"Yes."

"Walk me to the car?" He might get a kiss on her cheek. Or he might even get a brief one on that soft mouth. He wished he could stay and really comfort her. He might be able to convince her to let him. She was very vulnerable. But that wasn't what he wanted... to be a comforter. Let her heal first.

They went down the stairs to the entrance hall, she opened the front door and—*there stood Chas!*

He was just simply there!

He was dressed in a light suit, with dress shirt and tie. He looked formidable and, just like in the dream, he was *furious!* He ignored her and glared at Miles.

Miles stood there, smiled just a little ruefully and commented, "This is he."

"Yes." Both Chas and Amy had replied. She looked at Chas, but he was still looking at Miles. They were almost equal in height and weight, but Chas appeared somewhat larger.

Miles was rather enjoying himself. A little like an antelope sassily following a Cougar whose ears are laid back in temper. She introduced the two men—who did not shake hands.

"Leaving?" Chas encouraged Miles.

"I could always stay."

"Leave," Chas advised.

"You're being rude," Amy informed Chas.

"You can tell me about rude." He gave her a rude glance; so he knew, quite well enough, about being that way, all by himself.

Miles turned to Amy and opened his mouth to say goodbye, but Chas reached out and dragged Amy out of reach. Amy tried to pry Chas's fingers from around her arm. The two men looked at each other in a very electric silence.

Miles asked Amy, "Do you want me to stay?" And he put down his bags.

"No. Thank you, but he really isn't dangerous."

Chas overrode her statement. "Yes, I am."

"Are you trying to start something?" Miles asked Chas softly.

Chas's head came forward a little in that challenging-bear posture. "Are you the reason she left?"

Amy bristled. "I hadn't even met him until I came home."

Ignoring her, Chas advised Miles, "Don't clutter up the situation."

But Miles had been challenged. "I believe I'll stay. I don't like the way you're treating her. I'll stay until I know she'll be all right."

Then Chas smiled just a little. He parted his lips to say something, but Amy said, "For Pete's sake! *Both* of you leave! Out! Both of you!"

And Chas snarled at Miles, "See what you've done?"

That surprised Miles. "I've done? I was peacefully leaving, and you barge in and start throwing your weight around. You're the one who's upsetting Amy."

"She needs upsetting!" Chas ground through clenched teeth.

"That may well be." Miles recognized he hadn't a chance, so he might just as well help Chas. "I don't know the whole story, but she did say she'd lied to you."

Amy gasped as Chas asked, "She told you that?"

"Yes. And she said she was devastated, but not as bad as Hiroshima."

"Good grief!" Amy shrieked. "Out!"

Miles gave Chas his hand as he said, "Luck. Name the first one after me."

Amy shouted, "What are you doing to me?"

Miles smiled pacifically at her. "I'm helping. You have my card. Let me know how things come out. Understand?" If she didn't, he would be in touch. This might clear the air. The other guy was hostile and no real competition. She now knew that after Chas left, he was in the wings and waiting.

She glared at him.

With Chas glowering, Miles added recklessly, to Amy, "I believe you're a treasure." She would remember he'd said that after this Cougar left.

Chas hurried him along, "Goodbye, Clifford."

Miles gave Chas a long study, then he asked Amy, "Okay?"

She nodded woodenly.

Miles leaned over and kissed Amy's surprised cheek. He figured that should give Cougar something to think about. Then he smiled, rather pleased with himself, picked up his cases and left the two antagonists there, together.

Miles was barely out the door when Chas closed it after him with an emphatic thump. Then he glared down at Amy, who wouldn't look up at him. "All right. Tell me just why you took off that way? I suppose you have a reasonable excuse?"

"How did you find me?" Was that thin little voice really hers? She cleared her throat and straightened her spine, and again she worked at prying his fingers from her arm.

Before he released her, he tightened his fingers in a brief shake to show her it was his choice to let go. "Did you think I couldn't find you? If this is the beginning of a career as a thief, then you—"

"I didn't mean to keep it." She finally looked up at him with wide, earnest eyes. "I was going to mail it back to you." She fished the pearl from the front of her shirt. "Do you always carry two hundred business cards?"

His head was still forward in the threatening-bear stance. "I had them printed while I waited for Connie at the doctor's office."

"Oh." She had begun to take the chain off over her head. "I fully intended to leave your pearl with the note." The chain was tangled in her hair and his restraining hands.

"I was being symbolic in calling you a thief. Using men and discarding them is a kind of thievery. The pearl was a gift. If you'd left it with that stiff little note, I'd have lost hope."

"I worked very hard over that note." She defended as she gave up on removing the pearl for then. She finally led him into the living room overlooking the other end of the pool from the kitchen.

"I found the rejected versions in the wastebasket."

"How rude of you to find them." She had gone back to avoiding looking at him. There was a silence. "Did you explain to Sally?" She stood there.

"Yes." He finally sat down on one sofa. "Everybody missed you."

"I thought about you and wondered how . . . things went." Primly she sat on the sofa facing him.

"You could have stayed and found out," he said nastily.

There was a longer silence. She watched her fingers comfort each other in her lap.

He cleared his throat and asked in such a manner that she knew he wasn't talking about anything he really wanted to discuss, he was making a conversational bridge. "How, exactly, do political consultants work?"

And Amy, who had never told Chas very much, seized the opportunity to tell about herself. "A candidate pays for our expertise. We've done it all before."

"Is it fair? An expert against amateurs?" Naturally Chas would ask that.

"It's still up to the voter. You must be aware how few people actually vote? We do try. The registration push is done ahead with volunteers."

"Then what?"

"We help the candidate target issues, we learn where the local 'buttons' are, and which to avoid and which to punch. We become acquainted with the media people. We make up the advertising and schedule those. We supervise the raising of funds—direct mail and/or telephone, boiler-room type with volunteers. Events like breakfasts where the candidate can speak briefly. We sort out requests for speaking engagements, invitations, and arrange appearances.''

He sat watching her for a while, then commented, ''We are using a similar approach in localities where we'd like the Cougar products to become stronger. We couldn't count on volunteers, but there's that great resource—Cougar offspring.''

''Chas, you aren't into anything that pollutes or harms, are you? The fact that we now have wastes that are harmful for *two hundred fifty thousand years* simply appalls me.''

''We've been around a long time in this land, and we want it to last as long as we do, and on beyond us, I promise.''

She allowed her eyes to rest on him, finally. He watched her back, wondering what she was thinking. How bad was their rift. Could it be healed?

After a time, she inquired, ''Do you use your name in your company?''

It wasn't what he had expected her to say. ''No. Billy Cougar called it the Ace Manufacturing Company, and the title's come down unchanged.''

''The Cougar is such an American symbol. Dreyfus uses the lion, but the cougar is American. Why not consolidate under the cougar symbol? You could use cougar pins among your prize employees.''

''You're hired.''

She looked off, unseeing, frowning, concentrating. ''It would take other kinds of research. Politics is very interesting. I've met some wheelers and dealers, and the movers and shapers.''

''That's how you met Martin Durwood.''

"Yes. Why did you back me so quickly when I told Cousin Kenneth to watch out for him? Do you know him?"

"I'd heard tales of Durwood and, by then, I knew who you were and under what circumstances you'd probably met him. When you warned Kenneth, I was very pleased. It only confirmed what I knew about you. But it wouldn't have mattered if you hadn't been so quickly committed. It was already too late for you." Slowly, so not to spook her, he moved to her sofa.

"I thought I was anonymous."

"And safe?" He sneakily put his arm along the back of the sofa behind her.

"Yes. And I suffered so, thinking you might be hurt."

"Seeing Clifford here scared the hell out of me."

"You thought I'd gone sexually berserk? That no man was safe from me, now that I'd experienced you? That Miles was fleeing from my voracious body?"

He brought his other hand over to smooth her hair back from her face. "Is your body voracious?"

"Not as much as last week."

"Why is that?" He'd lightened his deep voice so it sent shimmers down her spine.

She swallowed. "A mysterious stranger has been slowly rubbing out voracious." He drew in a sharp breath, but she went on quickly, "I thought about you and wondered how . . . things went."

"I hope your bloody conscience gave you fits."

When he leaned and kissed her cheek, he very seriously excited her down the middle of her stomach, and she said sadly, "I felt terrible. I was afraid I'd hurt your feelings. I didn't know how to say goodbye."

"I should think not!"

In that sad little voice, she told him, "I had night-mares."

"I sweat a little, too. I didn't know where you'd run. Then I got here, and you opened the door right on cue, but you were with another man! With suit-cases! Ready to go God only knows where!"

"He was leaving."

"Did you sleep with him?"

"Good grief! I only met him last night!"

"You were in my bed that first day."

"Well . . ." She looked helpless to explain.

"Amy, about your 'using' me. There's something you need to know."

She confessed, "I set out deliberately to seduce you." She raised guilty eyes to his.

"Did you?" He smiled down at her.

"Yes. I figured if men could be womanizers, then I could be a man-izer."

"I see."

"I didn't mean to be so fast and crass. But there was only a limited time."

"Yes." He was grave, watching her.

"It was so easy!"

"Was I?"

"Oh, I don't mean you're loose," she assured him earnestly. "I just meant I was amazed how . . ." She looked at him, anxious not to offend him. "It . . . just . . . worked. I sort of waited around, and went along and it all worked out. As you know, you were my first."

"And last. What made you choose me?"

"Well, in the lobby when I was registering, I saw you."

"As early as that?" He very carefully moved her to him, with her head on his shoulder, and his free hand held hers.

"I had been considering an affair," she told him openly. "But I had never seen a man I really wanted, before. But then I saw you, and The Plan formed. After I overheard all the talk about Trilby's elusive family, I revised the title to The Relative Plan."

"Clever." He kissed her forehead, his breathing was a little quick.

"I thought so, too. At that time, I foresaw a long list of titles for my seductions. I thought I might put the titles next to the check marks on my closet wall."

"Closet wall?" He'd lost track.

"Instead of notching the bedpost, you remember."

"Ahhhh. Of course."

"When I made my move, you didn't blink an eye." That still amazed her.

"Are your parents home?"

"No. They've taken their friends, the Peckerels, to church then brunch. They won't be back until two or three this afternoon."

Chas looked at his watch. "You were saying I didn't react when you made your move?"

"No. I thought you might be startled, but you didn't react at all."

"That was when you . . . Show me."

"I'll have to lie down." She was excusing her conduct.

"Oh, yes." He rose and removed his suit coat and tie in wink of an eye. He'd unbuttoned the top several shirt buttons and was working on his cuffs by the time she'd arranged herself.

She moved until she was just so, then she looked up. "We were going to watch the film, remember? And... well, you have to lean over as if you're going to kiss me."

"This is just a tad narrower than the bed, move over a little. There. And I was like this?"

"Yes. And... ummmmm. Uhhhh. Ummmm. I didn't mean you actually had to kiss me."

"We're being authentic."

"Yes. Well. Then I put my hand right there and nudged your head closer. Ummmmmmm. Yes. Like that. And you acted the same way then! You weren't startled or anything."

Chas said, "You're very subtle."

"Thank you. What are you doing?"

Chas was involved. "Taking off your shirt."

"I know. But... Here, let me help."

"I need the practice." Chas was kneeling beside the sofa. He took off her shirt, lifting her and being very gentle. He discarded her shoes, undid her slacks and eased them off along with her lace panties.

When he stood up, and worked on the rest of his shirt buttons, she said, "I feel lazy, not helping."

"I like looking at you, lying there, waiting for me."

His voice was husky and deep. It sent thrills through her as she watched his body unsheathed from his clothing. He was awesome. While Miles had been beautifully made, Chas was awesome. "You worked hard for those muscles." She reached out a hand and ran it along his hard thigh.

"The family has lumber camps," he explained. "We all work our way through college, but they start us out in high school in what the elders call training.

All Cougars are muscled, because we're family and work cheap. The elders call it experience, but it's really just child exploitation."

He grinned at her. "When a boy is born in the Cougars, the elders all cheer. It's not that he's a male, it's just they have gained more cheap labor. Cougars have sons. The daughters are so rare that they're cherished. That's why I need you. I need some cherishing."

She touched him. She reached and put her hands on him as she watched his face. "Why did you have to come here? I'll never get over you now."

Chas was sympathetic. "I know."

"You're making this hard for us."

"Yes." He laughed low in his chest as he came down to her.

"Impossible." She agreed as she curled around him. "Ah, Chas."

He rolled on a condom and began to make exquisite love to her. She didn't have much chance to cherish him. He was so loving that she could only gasp and squirm as their hotly filmed bodies melded together, with their hearts thundering and their breaths ragged.

He murmured outrageous things to her, which she accepted as very serious. He meant them. He told her she was his, that they would marry and try for cherished daughters. They would all look like her. He would love her all his life and take care of her, while she cherished him.

He examined every inch of her, giving her his concentrated attention and his murmurs of appreciation. He drove her wild, as he trembled and shivered with his need, and waited. He kissed and touched and stroked and felt and kneaded and suckled and tongued, while she squeaked and dug her fingers into him and writhed, riding his passionate restraint.

When he finally took her, she convulsed in ecstasy, and he laughed in her pleasure as he rode her climactic shudders, reaching his own.

Lying spent, their hair sweat limp, their bodies cooling. He was inert and she was languid. She moved lazy fingers in his hair as she said pensively, "We're all wrong for each other. I really don't care for domineering men."

He moved the slightest little bit, only to press into her, then he said, "I'll change." But he said it so complacently that there was no conviction to his words. "We'll get married as soon as your parents get over the shock of meeting me."

"My father would be so pleased with you for a son-in-law, and my mother would adore you."

"If parental approval is a stumbling block, I can contrive for them to dislike me."

"Impossible." Then she asked earnestly, "How can you approve of me when I went to bed with you the first time I met you?"

"It wasn't the first time, it was a whole, discreet twenty-four hours after we met! It was meant to happen just that way. I knew we were meant to be, but you had this silly idea of shopping around."

"Tasting," she corrected.

"Whatever."

"How could you possibly have known this was serious with us?"

"I knew when you came into the lobby that first night. I had a hell of a time maneuvering so I could be in back of you when you gave your... false name."

"How did you know it was false?" She was a little indignant, lying there under his relaxed, contented body.

"No one named Abbott calls herself AAAbbott. Dead giveaway. When did you know I was the one for you?"

"I haven't yet accepted that. But out on the pier..."

"Yes. That's why you got the pearl instead of a sailfish."

Hesitantly she inquired, "A *sailfish?* They're enormous!"

"I would have hung it over your bed... as a reminder of me."

She laughed, still lying under him. "But, Chas, we aren't suited."

He shifted just enough to remind her where she was.

"Oh, there's no question we're sexually compatible," agreed the novice, "but our life-styles are quite diverse. You are a part of a large family, and I am used to a very isolated existence, and quite a selfish one. I was overwhelmed by all your family."

"There are many, many more of us."

"This whole situation is impossible." Then curiosity forced her to ask, "How did you find me?"

"Your license number."

"You traced me?"

"That first night."

"On *Wednesday?* We hadn't even met yet!"

Apparently she still didn't realize what exactly had happened to her, and how little she had to do with anything. Should he tell her? Make it clear? After he saw her come into the lobby, she had never had a chance. He relished lying on her soft body. She . . .

She was saying, "I'm not sure I could marry and leave the business world. My brain could dissolve. I believe you should forget marriage.

"I plan to compile a paper on our research on issues, problems, worries, grass-roots opinions for national election usage. It's a neglected resource. Our polls are more complete.

"However, I am willing to carry on an affair with you as long as you like. I travel, and we can meet wherever you can be. Perhaps you could marry a complacent, sharing woman, who would give you those sons for the mills, and I could be a great and good friend?"

He simply ignored most of what she was saying, "We'll bend to make you comfortable in our mass of Cougars, who are an untapped research resource for your paper and very willing to share their opinions and advice. You might even have an office to yourself. By mine." He nuzzled along under her ear. "But to get this plum space, and opportunity, you have to marry me."

"There's always a rock in the bed." She made her voice disgruntled.

He loved it. "So you compare me to a rock?"

"One way or another." She slid her hands over his deliberately knotted arms and the tensed muscles of his back. "What if I hadn't been a virgin? What if you hadn't been the first man I'd slept with? What if I had been a . . . Connie or a Sally."

"You are fated to be my wife."

"I didn't know how to say goodbye to you." It had been such a worry.

"Wasn't that some kind of clue to you? I didn't think you were that dense."

Her arms were up, her hands playing in his thick hair. "I know exactly what Billy Cougar was like. Just like you. They probably deported him from the U.K. for interfering and managing everybody. I'm not sure I can be your wife."

He blew softly along her shoulder before he breathed the words there. "You'll learn." He kissed her shoulder, rubbing his chin in little circles and touched his hot tongue to her skin in a tasting way.

"See? I think that's the attitude that got Billy deported. This has been so fast. I had no idea how devastating an affair could be."

"This isn't an affair. We are very seriously courting before we marry." He raised up from her soft body and braced himself on his forearms. "I love you, Amy."

"I strongly suspect that's exactly what's happened to me. I'm in love with you, too. I'd so hoped it was just a crush. It's awfully soon to be so committed to you, but I really am."

"I want you again. I'll want you all my life. But there's more. I want your mind. I want your companionship. I want you to share it all with me. As I will with you. We'll be partners, parents, a team. I'll wait until you understand it all. I'm very patient." He moved impatiently, pleasuring himself, loving her, possessing her, being possessed.

She still didn't realize it hadn't been an impulsive affair. It was as it had been meant to be. A very successful mating between a man and a woman, which would last for all their lives.

"Ah, Chas," she breathed the words. "I do love you."

"I know."

* * * * *

SILHOUETTE® Desire®

MAN of the Month 1995

Don't let the winter months get you down because the heat is about to get turned way up...with the sexiest hunks of 1995!

January: *A NUISANCE*
by **Lass Small**

February: *COWBOYS DON'T CRY*
by **Anne McAllister**

March: *THAT BURKE MAN*
the 75th Man of the Month
by **Diana Palmer**

April: *MR. EASY*
by **Cait London**

May: *MYSTERIOUS MOUNTAIN MAN*
by **Annette Broadrick**

June: *SINGLE DAD*
by **Jennifer Greene**

MAN OF THE MONTH...
ONLY FROM
SIILHOUETTE DESIRE

DREAM WEDDING
by Pamela Macaluso

Don't miss JUST MARRIED, a fun-filled series by Pamela
Macaluso about three men with wealth, power and looks to
die for. These bad boys had everything—except the love of
a good woman.

* * *

"What a nerd!" Those taunting words played over and over
in Alex Dalton's mind. Now that he was a rich, successful
businessman—with looks to boot—he was going to make
Genie Hill regret being so cruel to him in high school. All he
had to do was seduce her…and then dump her. But could
he do it without falling head over heels for her—again?

Find out in DREAM WEDDING, book two of the
JUST MARRIED series, coming to you in May…only in

Take 4 bestselling love stories FREE

Plus get a FREE surprise gift!

SILHOUETTE®

Desire®

A new series from Nancy Martin

Who says opposites don't attract?

Three sexy bachelors
should've seen trouble coming
when each meets a woman
who makes his blood boil—
and not just because she's beautiful....

In March—
THE PAUPER AND THE PREGNANT PRINCESS (#916)

In May—
THE COP AND THE CHORUS GIRL (#927)

In September—
THE COWBOY AND THE CALENDAR GIRL

Watch the sparks fly as these handsome hunks fall for
the women they swore they didn't want!
Only from Silhouette Desire.

Also available by popular author

LASS SMALL

Silhouette Desire®

#05684	*'TWAS THE NIGHT	$2.79	☐
#05697	DOMINIC	$2.89	☐
	The following titles are part of the Fabulous Brown Brothers miniseries		
#05830	A NEW YEAR	$2.99	☐
#05848	I'M GONNA GET YOU	$2.99	☐
#05731	A RESTLESS MAN	$2.89	☐
#05755	BEWARE OF WIDOWS	$2.89	☐
#05800	BALANCED	$2.99	☐
#05817	*TWEED	$2.99	☐
#05860	SALTY AND FELICIA	$2.99 U.S.	☐
		$3.50 CAN.	☐
#05879	LEMON	$2.99 U.S.	☐
		$3.50 CAN.	☐
#05895	AN OBSOLETE MAN	$2.99 U.S.	☐
		$3.50 CAN.	☐

*Man of the Month

(limited quantities available on certain titles)

TOTAL AMOUNT	$
POSTAGE & HANDLING	$
($1.00 for one book, 50¢ for each additional)	
APPLICABLE TAXES**	$_____
TOTAL PAYABLE	$_____
(check or money order—please do not send cash)	

To order, complete this form and send it, along with a check or money order for the total above, payable to Silhouette Books, to: **In the U.S.: 3010 Walden Avenue, P.O. Box 9077, Buffalo, NY 14269-9077; In Canada: P.O. Box 636, Fort Erie, Ontario, L2A 5X3.**

Name: _____

Address: _____ City: _____

State/Prov.: _____ Zip/Postal Code: _____

**New York residents remit applicable sales taxes.
   Canadian residents remit applicable GST and provincial taxes.   SLSBACK5

Silhouette®

COMING NEXT MONTH

#931 SINGLE DAD—Jennifer Greene

June's *Man of the Month*, Josh Penoyer, had no time for women in his hectic life. But his kids wanted a new mom, and they'd decided beautiful Ariel Lindstrom would be perfect for the job!

#932 THE ENGAGEMENT PARTY—Barbara Boswell

Always a Bridesmaid!
When Hannah Farley attended her friend's engagement party, she never thought she could be the next one walking down the aisle, *especially* with an arrogant yet sexy stranger named Matthew Granger....

#933 DR. DADDY—Liz Bevarly

From Here to Maternity
Working with redhead Zoey Holland was more than Dr. Jonas Tate could stand. But when he needed advice for raising his niece, he found himself asking Zoey—and *wanting* the feisty woman....

#934 ANNIE SAYS I DO—Carole Buck

Wedding Belles
Annie Martin and Matt Powell had been inseparable friends since they were kids. Now a "pretend" date had Matt wondering how to get his independent and suddenly irresistible friend to say "I do!"

#935 HESITANT HUSBAND—Jackie Merritt

Mitch Conover refused to fall for his new boss's daughter, no matter what the sexy woman made him feel. But Kim Armstrong wouldn't give up until she worked her way into his heart....

#936 RANCHER'S WIFE—Anne Marie Winston

Angel Davis needed a vacation—not a headstrong rancher named ay Ryder to boss her around. But it wasn't long before she fell little girl...and the stubborn rancher *himself!*

Announcing
the New Pages & Privileges™ Program
from Harlequin® and Silhouette®

Get All This FREE
With Just One Proof-of-Purchase!

- **FREE Travel Service** with the guaranteed lowest available airfares plus 5% cash back on every ticket

- **FREE Hotel Discounts** of up to 60% off at leading hotels in the U.S., Canada and Europe

- **FREE Petite Parfumerie** collection (a $50 Retail value)

- **FREE $25 Travel Voucher** to use on any ticket on any airline booked through our Travel Service

- **FREE Insider Tips Letter** full of fascinating information and hot sneak previews of upcoming books

- **FREE Mystery Gift** (if you enroll before May 31/95)

And there are more great gifts and benefits to come!
Enroll today and become Privileged!

(see insert for details)

 PROOF-OF-PURCHASE

Offer expires October 31, 1996